SAGA OF THE SIX WORLDS

CRADOC'S QUEST

CHERITH BALDRY

Kingsway

Chariot Books™
A Division of Cook Communications

Chariot Books™ is an imprint of David C. Cook Publishing Co.
David C. Cook Publishing Co., Elgin, Illinois 60120
David C. Cook Publishing Co., Weston, Ontario
Nova Distribution Ltd., Eastbourne, England

CRADOC'S QUEST
© 1989, 1994 by Cherith Baldry

Designed by Foster Design
Cover illustration by David Moses
First Printing, Revised Edition, 1994

Printed in the United States of America
98 97 96 95 94 5 4 3 2 1

Library of Congress Cataloging-in-Publication Data
Available upon request

First published in 1989 as *The Book and the Phoenix* by Kingsway Publications Ltd., Eastbourne, England
British ISBN 0-86065-729-9

Pronunciation of Some Names from the Six Worlds

Andarre	Andarre' (rhymes with "afar")
Baric	Ba'ric ("a" as in "cat")
Berard	Be'rard (like English "Gerard")
Ferelith	Fer'elith
Herrian	Herr'ian
Huon	Hoo'on
Lindor	Lin'dor
Rual	Roo'al
Rya	Ree'a
Tybalt	Ti'balt ("i" as in "fit")

To Adam

The Six Worlds

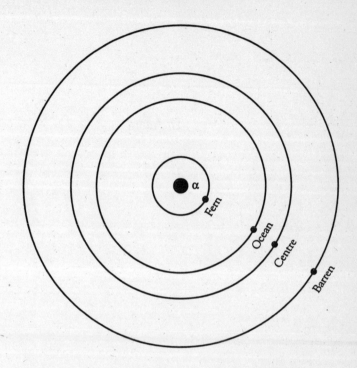

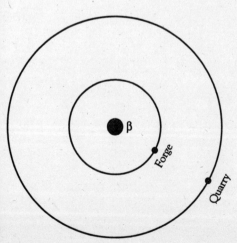

The Six Worlds and their two suns, Alpha and Beta, form a binary system. Beta takes several thousand years to make one circuit of Alpha.

This plan is not to scale.

1

They came in the hour before dawn. Cradoc and the other farm boys, still stupid with sleep, were stumbling from their beds above the stable. Down the rickety wooden stairs they came to the store where the animals' food was kept. At the foot of the stairs Cradoc stopped dead. The boy behind collided with him and cursed halfheartedly.

"Quiet," Cradoc said. "I can smell smoke."

For a moment they all listened. Then Cradoc edged open the door to the yard. Thick black smoke coiled through the gap. Cradoc hesitated before slipping outside. The sky should have been growing light, but the untidy line of rooftops was hidden by the dark covering of smoke. Cradoc groped his way across the yard to hammer on the door of the farmhouse. But before there was any reply, a confused shouting broke out behind him. A horse neighed and he heard the sound of trampling footsteps. Intruders were raiding the barn.

The raid was short, though Cradoc felt he had spent hours floundering around in the smoke. Half of his instincts told him to fight in defense of the farm. The other half told him to find somewhere safe until it was all over. Actually, he did neither. He tried to obey shouted orders without knowing whose they were, not knowing which of the obscure shapes around him was friend or enemy. With eyes stinging, he choked on the acrid smoke, blundered across the yard to where he could see flames spurting up from the cow barn, but encountered no one to help him or hinder him. He could do nothing. Then suddenly it was over.

Near silence fell, broken only by the crackle of flames. A faint breeze sprang up and drove off the smoke. The sky showed the light of a gray morning. Cradoc stood looking around him. The barn still burned. Huge piles of wet straw had been heaped around it to give off the smoke that had been the cover for the raid. The gates to the yard were broken down. Around him his companions stood, all momentarily silent, until the farmer abruptly recovered himself and began to yell his orders.

Not much later the fire was out. Cradoc, his eyes still stinging, was raking the straw away from the barn, spreading it and tramping on any hidden flames. A thin drizzle began and helped him in his task. By now they knew the damage. Half of the barn would have to be rebuilt. The raiders had driven off three of the best cows and the farmer's own horse. They had also pillaged the storerooms. No one remembered that Cradoc had discovered the raid and tried to give the alarm. Cradoc was not surprised.

As he bent over the rake, his eyes fixed on the smoldering straw, he gradually became aware of another sound—a faint hum that became a muted roar, filling the air. Cradoc straightened, scanning the sky above the rooftops. Shortly he saw it for a few seconds as it slipped down through the clouds and disappeared behind the huddle of farm buildings. It was on its way, he supposed, to the city—one of the great silver ships that came from Centre to Barren and the rest of the Six Worlds, bringing . . . Cradoc did not know what the ships brought, or why they came. But he still watched for them.

He stood now staring at the place where he had had the brief glimpse of the ship. At his feet, unregarded, a tiny bead of flame crept along the straw. Something was hurting inside him— something that was not the gnawing hunger he felt every day. He could not explain it. He only knew that he longed for something and did not have the power to say what it was.

He cried out sharply as the rake was torn from his grasp. It landed on his shoulders in a couple of sharp blows and was thrust back at him. Jerd, the overseer, stood in front of him.

"Dreaming, lad?" he asked savagely. "And the farm burning down around you? I wish I had time to dream. Staring at the ship, were you? Much good that will do."

CHAPTER 1

Cradoc muttered something apologetic and resumed his raking. But Jerd, who had now found someone to work off his bad temper, was not so easily placated.

"They have nothing to do with you, those ships," he went on. "You'll never ride in one, that's for sure. You'll stay here doing your proper job, or I'll know the reason why."

This time Cradoc's mutter sounded more rebellious, but it earned him no more than a stinging slap around the ear.

"Ships!" Jerd grumbled. "We'd be better off if there weren't any ships. They raid this world, see, like those fellows this morning raided the farm. They're rich and powerful on Centre. Oh, yes, they can do anything. But you never find them helping us here on Barren, do you? No. So don't let me catch you staring at them again. Do you hear?"

The last few words were punctuated by blows and ended with a thrust that sent Cradoc staggering.

"Get out of my sight!" the overseer snarled. "Get out to your work in the fields. Or do you want the birds to eat next year's crop so there's nothing left for the raiders?"

Cradoc fled without a word.

2

Cradoc trudged down the field path. Every few steps he heaved on the wooden clapper and the birds that scratched in the furrows fluttered up and alighted again a few yards away. His arms and his back ached. He was soaked through from the persistent drizzling rain. It was still early morning, but he felt as if he had been tramping for untold hours through the mud at the edge of the field.

To his left, shallow furrows scratched out of the poor soil stretched to a ridge, and beyond the ridge was the farm. Beyond that was the city, but Cradoc had never been there.

To his right was the forest. No one went into the forest. There were tales of the creatures that lived there—demons, they said, ghosts, and other things it was best not to ask about. Once a city had stood there, so they said, before the war that had destroyed it and so much else. You could still find its ruins if you were foolish enough to go and look. Perhaps the inhabitants still watched over it and guarded its secrets.

Cradoc would liked to have known the truth about the forest, but this morning he was too wretched to give it more than a passing thought. He did not know why. There had been a raid, but there were always raids. Jerd had beaten him, but that was not unusual either. For a while there would be more work and less food, but he had weathered such times before. Perhaps that was the cause of his trouble. Cradoc had never known any home but the farm, and he could see no escape from it.

"There must be more than this," he said to himself. "Life must be more than this."

Normally he was willing enough, and contented enough

with what could not be changed. But now a wild desperation was swelling inside him. The rest of his life, day after day of unremitting toil, no praise, and no improvement, and never, never any change at all, rose up in front of him like a great black wave.

His thoughts turned to the one person who seemed to offer hope—Father Huon, who lived in a hut on land that belonged to Cradoc's master. The farmer, who normally had a sharp eye to profit and loss, seemed to have a superstitious feeling about him, and so he allowed the hut, and a patch of ground for a garden, and, when one could be spared, the services of a boy. For some time now, the boy had been Cradoc.

Father Huon fed him, talked to him, had begun teaching him to read, and in particular had told him about the God who made all worlds. According to Father Huon, this God had once lived as a man, and even now He was somehow present in the world, helping, guiding, showing men how they should live. This morning Cradoc was in no mood to believe it.

If it were true, he thought, *we wouldn't live like this. Raids, beatings* . . . He lacked the words to explain what he meant to himself. *Even if God did make the world, He isn't interested in it anymore*.

Somewhere, just on the edge of sight, there was a flicker of golden wings. Cradoc came to himself, hastily swinging the clapper before the farmer or the overseer happened along and discovered his negligence. But something nagged at a corner of his mind. Golden wings? He looked at the field before him and the drab, brown birds of Barren. Golden . . . it was there again, in a thicket at the edge of the forest. Stealthily, Cradoc edged his way toward it. There was a flash of gold. Cradoc stopped dead, staring around him. Where? In the trees? The clapper fell from his hand, and he never realized it. He took a pace forward, another, skirted the thicket, and plunged forward into the forest.

At first the trees were widely spaced, and the going was easy. Part of Cradoc knew how stupid he was being. This was the forest, full of such evil things that no one had ever come back to tell about them. Even if the Old People still guarded their secrets, they would not be his for the finding. And when he returned—if he returned—there would be a beating for leaving his post. He stopped and looked back, and could still see the field and the cold sky through the trees. Above his head the gleam shone out again; he turned and continued his pursuit.

The forest was growing thicker, and the going became more difficult. Brambles tore at his tunic. He scrambled up and down steep banks, hauling himself up by roots and branches, slipping and stumbling in what had become a desperate urge to keep that tantalizing hint of gold in sight.

Sometimes he thought he had lost it altogether. Sometimes, briefly, he saw it better—a crest or a sweep of wing—before it vanished again. It was bigger than he had thought at first. He did not think anymore about why he was doing this, or what he would do if he caught it. He did not really imagine he could catch it.

At last he broke through a tangled mass of briars and stood still. Through the trees ahead of him poured a flood of golden light, as if the sun had sunk down into the forest. There was no sound but his own sobbing breath. He could not move. He felt inside him, but a thousand times more piercing, the pain he had felt when he gazed at the silver ship. He had never in his life been so terrified. And yet he wanted to go on feeling it, as if he had never in his life been so alive.

As he stood transfixed, a faint breeze seemed to spring up and brought with it a fragrance. Afterward he could never describe it—it was not flowers or spices, but more beautiful than either, and as clear as if a voice had said, "Come." Cradoc stepped forward through the barrier of trees.

He found himself in a wide clearing. The bird he followed towered above him. Its wingspan stretched from tree to tree. Golden light flowed out of it, but Cradoc was not blinded; he could see every feather etched in its brilliance. The plumed head and the great pinions streamed into flame. The head turned, and the jeweled eyes fixed on Cradoc. Then it vanished.

Cradoc stumbled forward, shouting.

"No! No! Come back!"

He tripped and fell, and lay pounding the earth with his fists and crying hoarsely like a small child in a rage. He could not bear the sense of loss. Gradually his cries sank to quieter sobbing, and at last, as exhaustion overcame him, to silence. He could taste leaf mold in his mouth, and it stung in his eyes. He sat up, bewildered, rubbing his face, and looked around.

The clearing was empty. He knew it would be useless to look for the bird. The only light was the cold light of day on Barren, filtering through the trees. He was suddenly afraid. He did not know his way back. He was not even sure where he had entered the clearing. And he did not know if going back now, to the inevitable beating, was even worth the effort.

But as he sat there, unable to summon the strength to move, he began to notice something else. The floor of the clearing was not just the usual expanse of moss and forest plants. It was raised up in strange knolls, in lines too straight to be natural, and arranged in a regular pattern. He had fallen over one of them. He reached out a hand and peeled away moss. Beneath it, crumbling as he pulled the plant away, was gray stone.

Instantly alert again, he was on his feet before he realized it. Yes, the knolls did run in straight lines, and the lines formed squares, as if here had been buildings—many buildings, or many rooms forming one building. Then it was true. Someone had once lived here, here in the forest—or rather, in a city that had existed even before the ancient trees.

"Before the Black Years," he said aloud. "Before the War."

Terror stabbed him briefly. Here if anywhere he might expect to find the demons, the Old People who would show no mercy to an intruder. Then he grew calm. The bird had been no demon. He was sure of that. He began to move around the clearing, searching. He did not know what he was searching for, but there must be something, for he knew now that the bird had brought him, and there must be a reason for it.

At first there seemed nothing but the fallen, crumbling stone. He wondered despairingly if he would have to strip away every scrap of moss before he could find what he was looking for. Then he found himself standing on what had been a paved floor.

Trees had thrust up through it, breaking up the slabs with their roots, and smaller plants had crept and twined among them. The stones that remained were broken and uneven, and at the foot of one of the greatest trees they had fallen away to reveal a hollow space. A scrap of rusted metal was visible inside it.

Kneeling, Cradoc tore away the plants and dead leaves. What he found had once been a locked metal box. But now it was so rusted that he could pull the lock away with no effort at all. Before he opened it he hesitated. What treasure might it be, to have been hidden so long, and to be revealed to him like this? His imagination failed. Shaking a little, he reached out and lifted the lid. Inside was a book.

3

Cradoc had seen a book before, so he knew what it was. It seemed quite natural to him that this one should have been so carefully preserved. He knew what had happened to books in the Black Years. Reverently he picked it up. Its cover had been soft leather, but now it was brittle and the pages were discolored; however, the close-set print was still legible to someone who could read it. Cradoc could not, but he knew who could.

"I'll take it to Father Huon," he said aloud.

He did not know the way out of the forest, but he set off in the direction he guessed to be right. He was not surprised (because he had realized that whoever was in control of this expedition—he was not) to find himself eventually on the edge of the trees—about a mile away from the post he had abandoned, and not far from Father Huon's hut. It was not yet midday, though he felt as weary as if he had spent several days wandering in the forest.

When he approached the hut, Father Huon was in the garden, hoeing vegetables. He straightened, leaning on the hoe.

"Good day, Cradoc," he began, and broke off. "My dear boy, you're filthy. Where have you been?"

Cradoc was oblivious of his appearance.

"I've been in the forest," he explained, holding out the book. "I found this."

Interested, Father Huon took the book and carefully opened it. Cradoc, watching eagerly, saw him go suddenly still. When he spoke, it was in an odd, quiet voice.

"Cradoc, I said you're filthy. Go and draw some water and clean yourself up." He did not even look at Cradoc as he went.

The well was behind the hut, so Cradoc could not see what Father Huon was doing next. When he had drawn one bucket of water and washed in it, he drew another for Father Huon's use and returned. Where Father Huon had been standing he found the hoe abandoned in the onion bed. He rescued it and put it away. Then he took the bucket, tapped on the door of the hut, and went in.

The hut was a single, large room with a sanded floor. At one end was a fire with Father Huon's cooking pots. There was a bed with a mattress made of rushes, a table and one chair, a couple of wooden stools, and an iron-bound chest which contained Father Huon's few possessions and his one, precious book.

Father Huon sat at the table pouring over the second book, the one Cradoc had found. Cradoc was shocked to see tears on his cheeks. He carried his bucket to the fire and went to stand beside him.

"Father—"

Father Huon reached for his hand and gripped it painfully.

"Cradoc—Cradoc, have you any idea, any idea at all, what this is?"

Cradoc shook his head.

"No, Father."

"No—no, of course not." He shook his head as if to clear it. "Bring a stool, boy. Sit down, and tell me everything."

Willingly Cradoc sat and related his story—his pursuit of the golden bird, the glorious vision of it in the clearing, its vanishing, his search, and the discovery of the book. Father Huon listened with a fierce concentration. He did not interrupt, and when Cradoc had finished he still said nothing. After a while, Cradoc timidly broke the silence.

"Father—what was it—the golden bird?"

Father Huon took a deep breath.

"Cradoc, you have seen—my heart fails me when I think what you have seen."

With an effort, he regained command of himself.

"I must begin at the beginning, Cradoc," he said. "You're not a stupid boy, but you are unschooled, and I have had too little time to rectify that. Now listen."

Cradoc leaned forward eagerly.

"You know, Cradoc," Father Huon went on, "men live on all the Six Worlds, but we did not come from any of them in the beginning—no, not even from Centre. We came once from another world, far away. Then there was a great war, and we lost touch with our home world. No ships or messages came, and our messages went unanswered. And after that came the Black Years."

"The Black Years, Father?"

"Yes. For when the link was broken, the people on the Six Worlds decided they would have no more to do with the war. They didn't even remember why they were fighting. It had dragged on for years. Everyone was sick of it, and terrified of it happening again. And some people in those days believed that the war had only begun because men knew more than was right for them to know. They thought if we could not build the ships or the weapons, peace would surely last forever. And so they began to destroy everything to do with learning. They smashed laboratories, they burned books—"

"Now I remember, Father—you told me about that."

"Yes. It's over now. Oh, there are still a few who would cling to the old ways, but most of us recognize it was a madness. Slowly we are trying to recover. On Centre not everything was destroyed— that's why they know how to send the ships. But even on Centre so much was lost . . . so much."

He sighed and fell into a reflective silence. Cradoc watched him for a moment and then asked, "But Father—this book?"

Father Huon roused himself.

"This book? This book, Cradoc, was the greatest loss of all." He laid a hand on it but did not open it.

"I have spoken to you of the God who made all worlds. In those days, before the Black Years, there were many churches on the Six Worlds and many books. One book in particular, that was brought from our home world, told the story of how God guided His people and how He lived in the world as a man. And it told us how we should live if we wanted to follow Him."

"You taught me this, Father," Cradoc said helpfully.

"Yes, but in part only. For in the Black Years, many churches were destroyed—there is no church on Barren now, and few even on Centre. And this book—the great book of God's Word—was utterly lost." His eyes lit. "Until now, Cradoc. Because that is what you have found. We have God's Word again, that was lost for so long."

4

Decisively, Father Huon got to his feet.

"It isn't, after all, as easy as that."

Bewildered, Cradoc watched him as he put up the shutters at the one window. Then Father Huon found a piece of cloth and carefully wrapped the book in it. He took his cloak from its peg and a staff that stood in a corner.

"Cradoc, you look tired out," he said. "But I dare not delay. Can you walk as far as the city?"

Cradoc gasped.

"You haven't eaten, I suppose," Father Huon went on, with a gleam of amusement. "Help yourself to some bread and cheese. You can eat it on the way. And don't look so startled. I haven't lost my mind."

Cradoc had wondered. Suddenly infected with Father Huon's haste, he grabbed bread and cheese from an earthenware crock, and was standing outside the door of the hut before he managed to stammer, "But Father—the farm . . ."

Father Huon dismissed the farm with a wave of the hand.

"We have more important things to see to. This book. Surely, Cradoc, after all I've told you, you must see that we can't keep this to ourselves?"

He closed the door, tucked the book under his arm, and set off down the path. Cradoc had to hurry to keep up with his strides. Between that and the food he carried, he had no breath to ask questions, but once they were well on their way, Father Huon began to explain.

"The book must be read and studied, Cradoc. There are men more learned than I who will be able to understand it. And we will know again, as we knew once before, what God's plan for us is. We will know God's will and be able to do it." He paused. "And that, Cradoc," he went on at last, "is not as easy as it sounds, either. This book of yours is going to cause the greatest upheaval in the history of the Six Worlds. More than the War. More than the Black Years. Oh yes," he replied to Cradoc's utter confusion, "nothing is going to be the same as it was."

They had reached the point where the path curved away from the edge of the forest and struck across a low shoulder of the hills. From here Cradoc was on unknown ground. He hesitated for a moment, took a breath, and then increased his pace to catch Father Huon, who had not paused.

"Any change is going to be for the better," he said to himself, thinking of the morning's raid. It seemed to have happened in another world. If Father Huon was right, he realized, it had happened in another world.

Coming up with Father Huon again, he asked, "What are you going to do with it, Father?"

Father Huon looked at him, faintly amused.

"Unschooled as you are, Cradoc, you have asked the one question that really matters. For as it is now, it is so . . . vulnerable. It could be lost again, or stolen, or burnt. There must be copies, Cradoc, many copies, spread throughout the Six Worlds so that everyone can read the truth for themselves."

"But how?"

"I told you we are recovering, slowly, from the Black Years. Books are being produced again. On Centre there are printing presses. My book that you have seen came from Centre. My lady Rya sent for it and gave it to me."

Cradoc nodded. Father Huon had often spoken of Lady Rya, daughter of their lord who lived in the city. He often went to visit her and talk to her.

"That book is about God, too," Cradoc said.

"Yes, *The Sayings of Our Lord*, but—it's a fragment, Cradoc, compared to this. It was put together from men's memories, trying to preserve what they could, when the original was lost. Useful, and very precious to me, but not important now."

CHAPTER 4

Cradoc must have looked shocked, for he smiled.

"Except as any book is important. But you're right, Cradoc, this is the one we must provide for now. It must go to Centre and be reprinted. I shall speak to my lord, and make arrangements to go at once. And I must—"

He stopped dead, and broke off what he was saying at the same time. Cradoc waited, wondering.

"I'm a fool," Father Huon went on, after a moment's pause. "If I go to Centre, that will arouse the sort of interest we must be sure not to arouse. There must be another way. . . ." His voice died away, and then he slowly smiled. "Cradoc, how would you like to take the book to Centre?"

For a moment Cradoc was silent, not sure if he had heard right, or if he had, what it would mean. At last he managed to say, "Go in the silver ships?"

"Yes."

"But . . . oh, no, Father, I can't. I have to go back. . . . I have to scare the birds."

Father Huon now looked definitely amused.

"I think we can say, Cradoc, whatever happens, you have scared your last bird."

Cradoc could not understand that properly, either.

"But Father, would they take me?" he asked. "And when I got to Centre—I wouldn't know what to do or where to go."

"Well, I shan't send you off with your mind a blank," Father Huon said, setting off again at the same brisk pace. "This has come at the right time. And I'm sure that's no accident. Lady Rya is about to be married to a lord of Centre. She is to leave Barren in a few days. You will go with her, as her attendant. I can arrange that."

"But I can't—" Cradoc began.

Father Huon overruled him.

"I shall give you a letter to Lord Herrian, who will be her husband. I know he is a friend of the church. You will give the book to him, and he will do the rest."

He paused and went on again.

"There is one thing, Cradoc. There may be danger. There are

still men who would return us to the Black Years, and others who are no friend of the church for reasons of their own. With all that in mind, Cradoc, will you go?"

Cradoc was still struggling with a vision of the silver ships, and a sudden, desperate longing for something that now seemed miraculously possible. But he still had to say, "You should go yourself, Father. It would be safer with you."

"No. No one will question your presence, but they might very well question mine. Besides—you haven't forgotten how you found the book? Can you doubt that you were chosen for this?"

Cradoc thought for a while, and then asked quietly, "What was it, Father? What did I see?"

"There's a legend—a very ancient legend, from our home world—about a miraculous bird they called a phoenix. There was only ever one phoenix in the world, and when it grew old it would burn itself upon a pyre. When the flames were out, in the ashes would be an egg, from which the phoenix would hatch again."

"So I saw . . . a phoenix?"

"More than that, I think. Because the phoenix died and was restored to life, as our Lord died and rose again, the phoenix became His symbol."

"Then it was—"

"Our Lord Himself. Yes, Cradoc. Or—no, I think you saw a part of Him, the part that He chose to reveal. Now do you see why I think you have been chosen for this?"

It was a long time before Cradoc could speak again. The idea was too overwhelming. He felt again a trace of the terror and delight he had experienced as he went forward into the clearing.

"Why should it be me?" he asked.

Father Huon smiled.

"Why not? You were in the right place. You are willing. And I believe you have courage, and a true heart." He paused, half-laughing. "Cradoc, I lacked faith when I said there was no church on Barren. I am the church, and Lady Rya, and others. Cradoc, you are the church."

It was late afternoon before Cradoc saw the city. It was built of stone, huddled within its walls. In the middle of it was a larger, towered building, that Father Huon pointed out as the citadel, where they were going. Cradoc felt somehow disappointed. He had never seen so many buildings all in one place before, but this was where the silver ships came, and he had expected something different, something marvelous . . . the walls of silver, perhaps. This looked ordinary. Then he reminded himself that perhaps these wonders were still to come on Centre, where the silver ships came from.

They reached the gates, and the guards, clearly recognizing Father Huon, let him enter without question. They scarcely glanced at Cradoc. The main street led steeply up to the citadel. Cradoc looked around curiously at the inns and shops on each side. And the people—more people than he had seen before, all looked unfamiliar. Then he was passing through the gates of the citadel, past more guards and into a wide, paved courtyard. From here they were passed from servant to servant—all very finely dressed, Cradoc thought, and all very respectful to Father Huon—until at last Father Huon was led off to Lord Berard, Lady Rya's father. Cradoc was left alone in a small room and told to wait.

He sat on a bench under the window and waited. He could see across the city to the fields beyond and a loop of the road he had traveled. For a few minutes he wished he could return along it. But he knew what lay at the end of it for him—the farm, the old life that he had longed so desperately to escape from. When he thought of that, he had the courage to face whatever lay ahead.

After a while the door opened again and a girl came in. She was about Cradoc's age, as tall as he, with golden hair in long braids. She was wearing a blue dress with a woven border. Awkwardly Cradoc got to his feet. The girl stayed by the door, looking him over.

"Well!" she said expressively.

"Are . . . are you my lady Rya?" Cradoc asked timidly.

"No." There was a world of scorn in the word. "I'm her cousin. She brought me up. My name is Ferelith."

Cradoc did not know what to do with that information.

"My lord wants to speak to you. He says you're to join the household. Though goodness knows why. Something to do with Father Huon, I suppose. Do you work for him?"

"No—no, not really. I used to . . . to scare birds. On the farm."

"Scare birds?" Ferelith gave a short, humorless laugh. "Well, by the look of you, I'm sure you were very good at it. We'll have to do something about you before my lord sees you."

She went to the door and called, and a servant appeared.

"Take this and have it washed—thoroughly washed," she instructed. "And find some decent clothes. Burn these others. I'll see him again when you've finished."

Cradoc followed the servant, feeling rather disgruntled. He had washed at Father Huon's well, and could not see what Ferelith was making such a fuss about. In the next hour he found out. His clothes were stripped off and he was scrubbed in scalding hot water until he felt as if his skin had been stripped off as well. Another servant washed his hair, then cut it and combed it. Wrapped in a towel, he was taken to another room where fresh clothes were laid out for him—clothes that he had never imagined wearing—fine wool and linen, and a silver pin to fasten the tunic at the throat.

There was a sheet of polished metal in the room and he looked at himself in it. He was surprised at what he saw. The only reflection of himself he had ever seen had been in a pool, or the bucket of water he washed in, and what he saw now was very different. A stocky figure, not tall, but firm. Brown skin, still scratched from the forest. Wide brown eyes. Short brown hair that was drying in curls. He started as another figure appeared in the mirror beside him.

"Well," Ferelith said. "At least you look more presentable now, Cradoc Birdscarer. You can come and meet my lord. Follow me."

She led him out, up stairs and down passages until he could not have found his own way back. Finally they stopped outside a door that was flanked by two guards. She tapped, and a voice inside called to them to enter. Cradoc stepped in and looked around wonderingly. He had never been in so fine a room. It was large, with a bright fire burning. The walls were hung with tapestries. At the far end was a table, spread with papers and writing materials. Father Huon was sitting there with another man, whom Cradoc supposed was Lord Berard. He was thin and gray-haired, and he was bent over the book with an expression of intense interest.

When Cradoc and Ferelith entered, Lord Berard got to his feet and came toward them with an absentminded smile, as if his thoughts were still occupied with what he had been reading.

"Thank you, Ferelith," he said. "You may go."

Briefly Ferelith looked as if she might have protested, but she dropped a curtsy in silence and withdrew, closing the door behind her. Lord Berard beckoned Cradoc closer to the table and stood for a moment looking down at him before taking his seat again.

"So this is the boy, Father," he remarked. "And your name is . . . Cradoc? Well, Cradoc, tell me how you found the book."

Stammering a little at first, but soon with greater ease, Cradoc told his story. When he had finished, Lord Berard remained looking at him in silence for a while.

"That is a wonder indeed," he said at last. "And on Barren . . . Barren of all places. Well, Father," he went on more decisively, "what you say is right, of course. The book must be printed. It must go to Centre. The boy is prepared to take it?"

Father Huon looked up at him, smiling.

"No second thoughts, Cradoc?"

Cradoc hesitated, took a breath, and made the final decision. "No, Father."

"Good. My lady leaves tomorrow, and you leave with her."

"Tomorrow!"

"Yes," Lord Berard said. "My daughter leaves for Centre and her marriage with Lord Herrian of Lindor. You will travel with her as her page."

"Yes, my lord." Hesitantly he added, "I don't know. . . . I'm not sure what she will want me to do."

"Ferelith will instruct you."

Cradoc was not sure how he liked the sound of that. He felt uneasy about the journey and unsure of himself. But he had no time to think about it, for Father Huon was taking his leave of Lord Berard, preparing to return to his hut. Cradoc was surprised that Lord Berard did not invite him to stay for the night; it would be dark before Father Huon could reach his home.

Before he left, Father Huon stood over Cradoc, resting his hands on his shoulders.

"God go with you, Cradoc," he said. "There will be danger, but I believe you can meet it and overcome it." He embraced Cradoc in a rare show of affection and took from around his neck a wooden cross that he always wore. "This is very old," he said. "I believe it came from our home world itself. You had better have it now." He passed the leather thong over Cradoc's head.

"Thank you, Father," Cradoc stammered, overcome by the gift.

Father Huon stepped back, smiling down at him. Then with a word of farewell he was gone.

Cradoc glanced at Lord Berard, expecting to be dismissed. But Lord Berard was standing rigid by the table, his face set, eyes fixed on the door as Father Huon's footsteps faded into silence. Then he took a long breath, seemed to relax, and looked at Cradoc.

"My daughter is to marry a lord of Centre," he said. His voice was quiet; something about it alarmed Cradoc. "She has never seen him. She is marrying him so that perhaps a little of the riches of Centre can be used to help our people here on Barren. She sacrifices her own happiness to help such as you, Cradoc from the farm. From tomorrow, unless her husband wishes, she will never see her home again. I may never see her again. Unless . . . for at the last minute, you come to me. You and this book. And at last we on Barren have something that Centre hasn't got. Something we can bargain with."

Cradoc took a step back.

"Don't be afraid," Berard told him. "I won't harm you. But you are not going to Centre. Nor is my daughter. I shall send this letter that Father Huon has written and one of my own, and this book will not go to Centre until the lords of Centre have paid me well for it."

"No!" Cradoc protested, angry and frustrated that he did not have the words to argue. "It's wrong. . . . it's too important. . . ."

"My daughter's happiness is important."

Desperately Cradoc fled toward the door.

"Father Huon! Father!"

As he dragged the door open Lord Berard rapped out a command and the guards outside barred his way. Cradoc turned, knowing he was trapped.

"Take him," Lord Berard said.

6

Cradoc's guards took him up endless flights of stairs to a small, bare room where they left him. As he heard the bolt being latched, he sank down despairingly on the room's one chair.

I've failed already, he thought. *I should have said something—made him see. . . . I knew Father Huon should have taken the book himself!*

He began to look around him, wondering about escape. The room was furnished with a bed, the chair, and a table. The only light, fading now as evening approached, came from a slit too narrow to squeeze through. Cradoc got up and peered out of it. He was high in one of the towers; the window overlooked a deserted courtyard. There seemed to be no way at all of freeing himself.

"I must get word to Father Huon!" he said aloud.

Even as he said it, he knew how impossible it was. Part of him wanted to fling himself down on the bed and sleep, and by the time he woke Lord Berard's message would be on its way to Centre. Cradoc's responsibility would be over. But he could not do it. However futile it was to stay awake, fighting exhaustion and battering at the problem, he could not give up.

"Lord Phoenix," he said, exasperation in his voice, "You didn't want this. If You want Your book to be printed and free for everyone, show me what to do, because there's nothing else I can do about it by myself."

Almost at once there was the sound of the door being unbolted. Cradoc started. It seemed miraculous; he had not really expected an answer to his plea. Light poured into his room, but it was not the fiery gold of the Phoenix—only Ferelith with a tray that held food, and a stand with a burning candle.

"What have you been up to?" she asked, setting her tray down sharply.

Cradoc moved away from the window.

"What do you mean?"

"I've never seen Lord Berard like that. You must have really made him angry—no, not angry exactly. . . ." She shook her head. "I don't understand it. I asked him if I should take you to my lady. He said you had displeased him and you would not be traveling to Centre."

"Is that all he said?"

"Yes. So I thought I'd better find out where you were and feed you."

"Thank you."

Cradoc was standing by the table where Ferelith had placed his supper. There was a bowl of soup, bread, cold chicken, and some fruit. He was ravenously hungry and the smell of the food was making it difficult for him to think clearly.

"It's all right," Ferelith said, softening slightly. "He won't hurt you. He's not like that. He's edgy just because of my lady leaving, but in a day or two he'll send you home to the farm."

"It's not that." Cradoc made a great effort. "Ferelith—don't go—listen to me. I've got to tell someone. . . ."

To his horror he found his voice shaking. Ferelith looked at him for a moment, frowning, and then suddenly smiled at him.

"All right. But is there any reason why you can't have your supper while we talk?"

She took an apple from the tray and sat on the bed to eat it, looking up at him expectantly. Cradoc brought the chair to the table and began to eat his supper. At the same time he told (for the third time that day), the story of the Phoenix and his discovery of the book.

"It should be printed," he finished, "and copies sent to all the Six Worlds. Father Huon said so. But your Lord Berard is going to keep it and make the lords of Centre send their help to Barren before he'll give it up."

"So Lady Rya need not go to marry Lord Herrian," Ferelith said.

She had listened to him in utter stillness, her half-eaten apple forgotten. Now she was frowning once again, and said no more. Cradoc realized how hopeless it was. Ferelith, like Lord Berard himself, would not want to see Lady Rya forced into this marriage.

"It's wrong, can't you see . . ." he began.

"Oh, it's wrong," Ferelith agreed crisply, seeming to snap out of her thoughtful mood. "Of course it's wrong. The only question is what we're to do about it."

She bit into the apple again.

"Then you'll help me!" Cradoc exclaimed. "But Lady Rya—"

"My lady is going to Centre to marry Lord Herrian. He fell in love with a picture of her—can you imagine that? Of course, no one has bothered to show her a picture of him. She's marrying him so she can help her people. Of course she's afraid, and of course she doesn't want to leave her father. But she knows it's right. And if she knew about the book, she would know it's wrong to keep it."

"Then if you tell her—" Cradoc hazarded.

Ferelith shook her head.

"No. Oh, it would work. If she knew, she would insist on going to Centre and taking the book with her. But she would know about it then, Cradoc, and she would be in danger. Father Huon told you there would be danger, and even I can see that he was right. There must be another way."

They sat silently thinking. Cradoc finished his supper, reflecting on the strangeness of being allied with Ferelith, whom he still found intimidating. It was not long before she got to her feet and began collecting his supper dishes.

"It's quite easy, after all," she said. "I can let you out of here. You go and tell Father Huon. He can stop my lord from being so stupid."

Cradoc hesitated. The thought of his freedom was wonderful, and the thought of handing back responsibility to Father Huon was even better. But he could see the flaws in the plan.

"I don't know. . . ." he began, reluctant to contradict Ferelith.

"What don't you know?"

"If it would work. It's dark now. It will take me hours to get to Father Huon and hours to get back here. Lord Berard might have sent his message to Centre by then. Or even if Father Huon came in time, Lord Berard might not listen to him if he still has the book."

Ferelith stared at him.

"You're saying we should take back the book?"

"Yes."

He caught on her face what might have been a fleeting look of respect.

"Well, you're no coward, Cradoc Birdscarer, I'll say that for you." She picked up the tray. "All right. I can see your point. Come on."

Breathless at the turn events were taking, Cradoc followed her. There was no guard on the door of his room, but one sat on a stool at the head of the stairs and got to his feet as they emerged.

"My lord wishes to speak to the boy," Ferelith explained, and sailed past him with her head in the air.

Cradoc followed, and to his relief the guard made no protest.

Ferelith led him down the tower stairs, dumped her tray in an alcove on the way, and finally brought him to the door of Lord Berard's rooms. The guards had changed since Cradoc's imprisonment.

"My lord's still at supper," one of them told Ferelith.

"That's all right. We'll wait."

Like the first guard, they made no protest.

"Now . . ." Ferelith began, when they were inside and the door safely closed, "he would have left it here, I think, but where. . . ."

She darted to the table and began turning over the papers.

"What did it look like?"

Cradoc told her, half distracted, and broke off to say, "But Ferelith, he'll know—even if I get away and take the book to Father Huon—your lord will know it was you."

"Well, of course he will," Ferelith snapped. "Don't be stupid. It doesn't matter. He won't hurt me, you know. He's a good man." Suddenly she began to sound fierce. "He's a good man and I won't have you think any different. He's just . . . he can't bear it, losing Rya. When it's over, he'll realize. So you don't need to worry about me."

She abandoned the table and went over to an iron-bound chest by the wall.

"You might try to help," she added irritably. "Don't just stand there gaping."

Cradoc had begun to look around him wondering where he could search when he heard the sound he had been dreading all along. The door was opening. He spun around. Behind him he heard the thud of the chest's lid falling closed. In the doorway stood Lord Berard.

7

Berard strode forward into the room and grasped Cradoc by the arm. Cradoc did not dare to move or speak. Beside the chest, Ferelith stood erect, white-faced.

"Well?" Lord Berard asked.

No one answered him.

"Well?" he repeated. "Ferelith, what are you doing? Did I order you to have anything more to do with this boy?"

"You didn't tell me not to," Ferelith replied. "I went to take him some food."

"And then?"

"And then he told me about the book."

Lord Berard sighed deeply. He released Cradoc and went to sit at the table facing Ferelith.

"My dear," he began, and his voice no longer sounded angry, "I can understand how you feel—your idealism, your wish for the book to be printed. And it will be—it will. But not until the lords of Centre have given us what we ask. Ferelith, do you want your lady to make this marriage?"

He was speaking so reasonably now that Cradoc was terrified—more terrified than if he had raged and threatened. *She'll agree with him,* he thought. *She'll agree, and the last chance will be gone.*

"My lady chose the marriage," Ferelith said, slowly, as if she were thinking out her reply. "She chose it because she felt it was right. She felt it was what God wanted her to do. If you stop her without explaining, you're treating her like a child. You ought to tell her and let her decide."

Lord Berard jerked to his feet again.

"No!"

"No." Ferelith flushed, and stepped forward so she was almost close enough to touch Lord Berard. "No, because you know she would still do what she thought was right. Well, my lord, if you don't tell her, I shall."

"You can't. I won't let you."

Cradoc, listening, could hardly believe what was happening. Not only was Ferelith supporting him, daring to oppose Lord Berard, she was winning her argument.

"And how can you do that? Shut me away like Cradoc? But my lady will ask for me. What are you going to tell her if I'm not there?"

Lord Berard suddenly groaned and covered his face with his hands. Ferelith touched his arm gently.

"I'm sorry, my lord," she said. "I know how you feel. But this book—if it is the true Word of God—we must share it. It isn't ours to bargain with, not really." She hesitated and then went on, "My lord, you have served God all your life. You taught my lady and me to serve Him too. You know—"

"Yes, yes," Lord Berard interrupted, not looking at her. "Very well. You shall go tomorrow—you and the boy and Rya." He turned to her at that and added, "But you tell her nothing of this. Do you understand? Nothing."

He crossed the room to another chest under the window and took out the book. It was still wrapped in the cloth Father Huon had provided. He thrust the bundle into Ferelith's hands.

"Take it and go. The letter is there too. Take it. I don't know why I ever thought—"

His voice failed and he turned away. Ferelith hesitated, stretching out a hand to him that he did not see. Then she went to the door, motioning to Cradoc for him to follow. Once outside and a few paces down the corridor, out of the scrutiny of the guards, she stopped and let out a long sigh.

"Oh!" She shook herself a little. "I'm glad that's over!"

"I thought you were—"

Cradoc broke off. He had no words to express his admiration.

"Don't be ridiculous," Ferelith retorted. "I told you he wouldn't harm us. But Cradoc—don't you see? I made him give us the book. If I'd left things alone, my lady wouldn't have to go to Centre tomorrow. If she's unhappy, it's my fault. She and my lord Berard— they're all the family I've ever had. I owe them everything. And now—" She paused and then added miserably, "I've always told her everything, but I can't tell her this."

There was nothing that Cradoc could say. He was relieved when Ferelith seemed to recover and resume her former briskness.

"You'd better go back to your tower room for the night," she instructed him. "And take that with you."

She held out the book to him.

"I'd rather you kept it."

"Maybe, but I can't. My lady's maid is packing my things, and I can't be sure she wouldn't find it. It's all right. Nothing else will happen now. I'll come and see you early tomorrow and take you to my lady."

Cradoc had to agree. In fact, he was too worn out to worry. Soon he was asleep in the little room that was no longer a prison.

Ferelith kept her promise and roused him early the next morning. She took him to Lady Rya's apartments after a short but thorough course of instruction on how to behave. Among other things she told him that he was taking the place of the boy who had been Rya's page. He had agreed to go with her to Centre, but did not really want to leave his family. That made Cradoc feel better since he was being useful to Rya, not just deceiving her for the sake of the book.

He already admired Lady Rya, knowing the step she was prepared to take for the sake of her people. And he admired her even more when he met her. She was small, golden haired, and beautiful. Even Cradoc could understand how Lord Herrian had fallen in love with her picture. She was graceful and laughing. But there were moments when the laughter died and Cradoc caught sight of a deep apprehension at the thought of her new life.

Later that morning he joined Lady Rya's attendants to go to the landing-ground. This was on the other side of the city—a flat plain with nothing visible on it as far as the eye could see.

"Where is the ship?" he asked Ferelith.

"Don't you know anything?" she retorted. "The ships that land here are only scouts or cargo ships. My lady will use the teleport."

"What's that?"

Ferelith unbent a little.

"I don't really know. I mean, I don't know how they do it. They just . . . step out of nothing. Look."

A few yards ahead of the party there had appeared a shimmering curtain of light a little bigger than a doorway. A man stepped out from it. Cradoc could not restrain a gasp. The man, wearing a gray and silver uniform, came forward and spoke quietly with Lord Berard.

"That must be the captain of the ship," Ferelith murmured.

The conversation was brief. Lord Berard looked tired and strained, but no more than could be explained by his saying farewell to his daughter. When he had spoken to the captain, he turned to Rya and held her hands for a moment saying nothing. Then Lady Rya embraced her father and stepped forward toward the iridescent curtain. For a second she hesitated. Then she lifted her skirts and went through, her head held high.

Her maid followed. Ferelith grabbed Cradoc's arm.

"Come on."

He had a moment of wild panic; then he was moving forward. As he passed through the curtain there was a short tingling sensation. He stopped dead as he found himself standing at the end of a short passage with gleaming metal walls. At the other end, Rya and the other women stood beside another man in uniform at a bank of controls. The captain, following Cradoc through the curtain, gave him a gentle push.

"Go on, lad," he said. "Welcome aboard."

Bewildered, Cradoc joined the others. He was, he had to believe, on board one of the ships, but it was not soaring through the sky as he had imagined it. He was disappointed and yet ill at ease because although he felt no sense of wonder, everything was too strange. A crewman's touch on his shoulder startled him.

"Come on. I'll show you your cabin."

Though he was reluctant to leave Ferelith and the others, he followed the man down corridors of the same gleaming metal. The crewman seemed friendly, but Cradoc was too nervous to respond. Eventually the man stopped in what seemed just another part of the corridor. But then he touched a button and a section of the wall slid back to reveal a small room beyond.

"There you are," the crewman said, and added when Cradoc did not move, "go on. It's yours, for the journey. I should unpack, if I were you. Your lady will send for you soon, I daresay."

He withdrew as Cradoc went inside and looked around him. The room seemed bare. There was a bed and table built into the walls. The chairs were shaped in a way that looked odd and angular to Cradoc, but felt comfortable enough when he sat down to try them out.

The opening to the corridor gaped at him. Seeing another button on the inside wall, he touched it. The door slid obediently across. Cradoc could not stop himself from trying the mechanism again to make certain he could get out when he wanted to. Sure that he could control it, he suddenly found himself grinning delightedly. There were wonders here, if not quite the ones he had expected.

Setting down his bundle of possessions, he began to explore his surroundings. There were other buttons set in the walls. One revealed a place to store clothes. Another held a tiny washroom where water, instead of being laboriously hauled from a well, squirted out at a fingertip's touch. Remembering how Ferelith and the castle people were unaccountably fussy about washing, he gave himself a rapid scrub and unpacked his spare clothes. He was wondering about the best place to store the book and Father Huon's letter when a crackling noise behind him made him start and turn.

The noise had come from a grille in the wall. It was followed by Ferelith's voice. It was distorted, but not enough to hide her huge sense of enjoyment.

"Hello, Cradoc Birdscarer. Are you having fun?"

"Well . . . I'm not sure—" he began, but her voice cut into his last words.

"I can't hear you, you know. Unclip the panel under the grille and press down the red switch."

Fumbling a little, he managed to follow her instructions.

"Ferelith?" he said cautiously.

"Oh, there you are. I'm speaking from the flight deck. The Captain wants you here."

Cradoc was not sure what the flight deck was, and he had no idea how to get there. But Ferelith was already explaining.

"Go out of your room and turn right. You'll come to an elevator—a door with a red border. Go in there and press the green button. That's all. Hurry."

The grille went dead. Cradoc stared at it for a moment and then tidily replaced the panel, all the while thinking over Ferelith's instructions. She sounded quite at home—expert, in fact—while he scarcely understood what he was supposed to do. He had better do as he was told, he reflected. He wondered again what to do with the book. He had no way of carrying it with him without everyone seeing what it was. Even on board this ship there might be danger. At last he thrust it under the bedcovers and smoothed them down again so nothing could be seen. Then he opened his door and ventured out.

He found the elevator door without any trouble. Inside was a small, square space with a control panel on the wall. It held a bewildering selection of buttons, but fortunately only one was green. He touched it. The door slid shut and there was a faint jerk. Somehow, although there was nothing to be seen, he had the sensation of traveling at high speed.

Another jerk and the door opened automatically. He stepped out and suddenly clutched at the door frame, for he thought for a moment that he had launched himself out into the night sky. Then he realized that he was standing in an open space, circular, dominated by what seemed like a vast window looking on the stars. White light stabbed at him from a thousand directions with a brilliance he could never have imagined on the surface of Barren. He stood lost in wonder.

At last he was roused by a voice speaking his name. For the first time he noticed that the segment of the flight deck nearest to him was occupied by panels of switches and flashing lights, and attended by crewmen. Rya was standing near one of them, beside the captain who was explaining something to her. Ferelith was also there. It was she who had spoken and she was beckoning to him.

"You found your way, then? Don't look so terrified, nothing is going to bite you."

"Have you traveled like this before?" Cradoc asked her.

"No, never."

"But you seem so . . ."

He could not find quite the right words, and he was still rather nervous of Ferelith. She shrugged.

"Well, sometimes some of the officers dine with my lord Berard, so it's not quite strange. But the Captain told me what to say to you." She paused, looking around her, and then breathed out softly, "It's marvelous."

Cradoc nodded agreement, but she was not looking at him. His eyes went back to the stars outside. He caught his breath in a gasp of pure terror as the blazing light suddenly seemed to streak towards them. One star in particular grew in size until Cradoc thought they would be engulfed in the white furnace. Then the movement ceased and he let out his breath. He still could not drag his eyes away from the quivering sphere of light that filled his vision.

"It's not real," Ferelith said, sounding as if she too had been shaken by it. "At least, it is, but it's not as close as that. That's not a window, Cradoc, it's . . ." Now she too was looking for words. "It's a kind of picture. And they can move it around and look closely at the parts they're interested in. Look. It's moving away now."

Cradoc watched, relieved as the screen returned to normal. What they were seeing, he realized, was part of a demonstration for Rya's benefit. It had left him feeling slightly sick and disappointed. He had liked the idea of gazing directly out on to the stars.

"We can look out," Ferelith said, as if she had read his thoughts. "They call it the observation deck. We'll go there later, but if you ask me, it's time someone said something about food."

His life on the farm had made Cradoc appreciative of his meals, whatever they might be. But he was relieved that the food he was offered shortly afterward was not very different from what he had been used to—or at least what he had eaten in Lord Berard's citadel.

However, when the meal was over, there were duties to be performed for Rya. It was not until some days later that one of the crew took him with Ferelith to the observation deck. By this time Cradoc was becoming used to the ship. He no longer started with astonishment at each new experience. But this was still wonderful. He and Ferelith stood together on a railed platform before a great sweep of transparent material. It was all that separated them from the soft darkness of space pierced by innumerable points of light.

There was no sensation of movement. The ship seemed to be floating lazily in the void. Suddenly it seemed to Cradoc that Barren and all the worlds, even Centre itself, were little floating specks—no more than dust in the vastness that surrounded them. His world had once stretched no further than the boundaries of the farm. Now he raised his eyes and saw the immensity of the universe. A sudden doubt seized him.

He turned to Ferelith.

"Ferelith—all this . . ." he began, stumbling over words in his efforts to find the right ones, "it seems so much. Does it really matter, what we're doing?"

She looked at him in silence for a moment.

"You know it does," she replied quietly. "Big doesn't mean important. Cradoc, your book matters more than anything."

Cradoc sighed. If Ferelith were right, the book meant more than the ship and all its marvels—more than the expanse of space through which they traveled—more than all the treasures of the Six Worlds. He had to accept it. But it made him wonder even more that he should have been the one chosen to guard it.

There came a day when he was summoned once more to the

flight deck. Rya and the others were already there. In the viewing screen he saw a turning sphere, blue and green and golden with a swirl of cloud, hanging in the darkness like a jewel. He was learning. He realized that he was looking at a world.

"That's Centre," Ferelith told him.

8

Cradoc stepped out of the teleport into blazing sunlight. He had left Barren at the beginning of its cold, reluctant spring. Here on Centre it was high summer. He stood in a large courtyard. Ahead of him steps led up to a row of columns with white walls beyond. A group of people, brightly dressed, were waiting there. Cradoc glanced at Rya. She stood white-faced, not moving. Then a young man detached himself from the group among the columns, ran lightly down the steps, and approached the travelers. He was not tall, but quick moving, with a bright, open face and reddish-brown curls. Rya took a step or two hesitantly toward him. He took her hands and bent his head to speak to her quietly. After a moment, Rya's set expression dissolved into a faint smile. The young man led her back toward the columns.

Since Rya's maid had stayed to see to the luggage, Cradoc and Ferelith were left alone in the courtyard. Ferelith was furiously rubbing her eyes.

"Well, that seemed all right," she said in a choked voice. "I'm not crying, Cradoc Birdscarer, and don't you dare say that I am."

She sniffed loudly, blew her nose, and put her handkerchief away.

"So that was Lord Herrian," she went on. "I suppose he'll do. But are we to be left standing here in the middle of this courtyard all day?"

They turned and looked around. The teleport entrance had vanished and all they could see was an arched gateway, manned by guards. There was no one else in sight. Then someone spoke behind them.

"Are you my lady Rya's attendants?"

It was a languid, disdainful voice. Cradoc and Ferelith turned. The speaker was a young man—no, Cradoc realized, a boy no older than himself—elaborately dressed in a tunic of stiff, embroidered silk. Heavy, dark curls framed a pale face with an arrogant expression. His critical gaze made Cradoc feel suddenly clumsy and dishevelled.

"I'm Rya's cousin," Ferelith said sharply, making Cradoc guess that she felt the same. "This is her page. His name is Cradoc. I'm Ferelith." The boy bowed his head.

"You're most welcome to Centre and to Lord Herrian's house," he said, though for all his courtesy there was no welcoming note in his voice. "My lord asked me to show you to your rooms. If you'll follow me. . . ."

He turned back toward the building and led them along the columns and through a door at the far end. Cradoc and Ferelith followed, exchanging glances. Their guide did not seem to think conversation was part of his duties.

After a while, Ferelith asked, "Are you Lord Herrian's page? What's your name?"

He gave her a cold look.

"My name is Torquil," he replied after a moment's pause. "I am my lord's harper."

He half opened a door as they were passing it and told them, "Your lady will live here."

They saw a small anteroom with a larger apartment beyond it. It had doors that opened on to a garden. After allowing them a brief glimpse, Torquil closed the door again and led them up a short staircase.

"Your rooms are here."

He opened one door and motioned to Ferelith to enter. Cradoc's room was a little further down the passage. Cradoc went in and put his bundle on the bed. Ferelith, who had followed, stood looking around her.

"This is nice," she said appreciatively. "We should be comfortable here."

"I hope so," Torquil said, and added dismissively, "though I don't suppose you'll be staying long."

Ferelith turned on him.

"Why not? We shall stay just as long as our lady needs us."

Torquil shrugged.

"I think Lady Rya will find herself better served by attendants who know the ways of Centre."

Ferelith stepped toward him, her eyes blazing.

"Lady Rya will prefer people around her who know her ways. And if you or your lord think I'm going to leave her here among strangers, you can think again."

Cradoc guessed she was close to tears, and he knew how she would hate to cry in front of the supercilious Torquil.

"Ferelith," he said peaceably, "you know my lady would never—"

"Don't you start!" she exclaimed. "Leave me alone. I don't know what you think you know about it, anyway, Cradoc Birdscarer."

She flounced over to the window and stood staring out. Torquil was looking amused.

"Birdscarer?" he asked. "Really? Is that how you served your lady? Strange customs you have on Barren. Still, I'm sure we can find you a few birds to scare here—if you really want to."

"I'm not here to scare birds," Cradoc replied, beginning to feel angry on his own account.

"No? Then what are you going to do? It sounds a most arduous task. I don't suppose it left you much time for learning to do anything else."

That was so close to the truth that Cradoc did not know how to reply. He stood looking at Torquil's small, contemptuous smile. On the farm less insult than this would have been settled by fighting. But Cradoc already knew he could not behave like that here. He was sure he could defeat Torquil easily, but that would have given him no satisfaction. And he did not have the skill to defend himself with words.

"I can serve my lady—" he began, but Torquil interrupted him.

"You can have no idea of how to live in a civilized household.

I'm surprised my lady put herself to the trouble of bringing you here from Barren."

Suddenly Cradoc's fury blotted out all discretion.

"I've a good reason for being here," he insisted. "I've been sent with this."

He fell on his bundle of possessions, and pulled out the book.

"Look at that!" he said. "It's the most important book in all the Six Worlds. Look at it!"

"Cradoc!" Ferelith exclaimed.

She had turned from the window and was staring at him in horror. But Cradoc was too inflamed by his fury to understand yet what he had done. Meanwhile Torquil had moved forward, taken the book, and was delicately flipping through the pages.

"Do you see what it is?" Cradoc asked.

"I see what it says it is. Most impressive." He did not sound in the least impressed. "And what do you propose to do with it?"

He handed the book back to Cradoc, and fastidiously dusted off his fingers. Frustrated, Cradoc realized that the gesture had gotten him nowhere. He realized, too, that he had just been exceptionally stupid.

"It was supposed to be a secret—" he began helplessly.

"Oh?" Torquil's brows lifted. "Then you aren't doing too well, are you? Don't worry. Perhaps you're better at bird scaring. In any case," he went on, "I can't see what all the fuss is about. These old tales are all very well, of course, in their place, but—"

"Old tales?" Cradoc interrupted. "You mean you don't believe it?"

"Does anyone? Anyone of intelligence, that is?"

Cradoc thought of Father Huon, of Rya and her father, and could not speak.

"My lady believes it," Ferelith interposed. "And Lord Herrian."

"I can't speak for your lady, of course. As for Lord Herrian . . ." Torquil waved a hand airily. "He gives his gracious protection to those who cling to the old ways. But as for believing . . ."

"I don't believe you—" Cradoc was beginning, but Ferelith interrupted him.

"Ignore him, Cradoc. He's just trying to upset us. He's enjoying it. You can see he is."

"Oh, I am," Torquil said silkily. "In fact, I can't remember when I've enjoyed a conversation more. But I regret I have other duties. If you need anything, please ask."

He bowed mockingly and went out of the room. Cradoc and Ferelith stood looking at each other, listening to his steps dying away down the corridor.

Cradoc put the book back in his bundle, sat down on the edge of the bed, and buried his head in his hands.

"I knew I would make a mess of it," he said. "Father Huon should have come himself."

"It wasn't your fault."

He was so unused to Ferelith's being sympathetic that he looked up, startled.

"At least," she added, "it was as much my fault as yours. I shouldn't have let him upset me in the first place. What does his opinion matter anyway, the little . . . Oh, I should like to scratch his eyes out—if I were an eye-scratching sort of person—which I'm not. And I'm sorry I said that about bird scaring. It just gave him a chance to be nasty. I won't call you that again."

"I don't mind when you do," Cradoc told her, rather to his own surprise. "And I'm not ashamed of it—not really."

"I know. Oh," she went on furiously, "I should have had more sense. Only—well, I've been upset ever since this started— this marriage with Lord Herrian. I've been worried about her. Especially since I made my lord Berard send you with the book. And now it looks as if it might be all right—I'm not myself today, and that's all there is to it."

Cradoc put out his hand and felt the shape of the book in his bundle. He was beginning to feel rather sick.

"I told him, Ferelith," he said. "He's seen it. He knows all about it."

"And he'll talk about it."

"If we went to look for him and explained properly and asked him—"

"No. You saw what he's like. He'd be more likely to talk then, just for spite."

"Then what?"

He spoke despairingly, not really expecting an answer. But he might have known that the practical Ferelith would have something to suggest.

"Pass it on. Now. Find Lord Herrian, give him the letter and the book. If he can't protect it, no one can. And order Torquil to be quiet, if necessary."

"You think we should tell him—about Torquil?"

They both thought that over. Neither of them was particularly proud of the episode.

"If you have to," Ferelith said at last. "See what he means to do first."

"All right." Cradoc got off the bed and consciously straightened. "I'll go and find him now."

Before he could leave the room, however, there was a step in the corridor—a different step from Torquil's, swift and springy. Its owner was humming a jaunty tune. At the door, the steps and the humming stopped, there was a tap, and Lord Herrian himself appeared. Ferelith dropped a curtsy and Cradoc would have knelt, rather clumsily, but Herrian prevented him.

"Never mind that," he said, smiling. "It's Cradoc, isn't it? And Ferelith? Welcome to Centre."

For the first time they actually felt welcome.

"Ferelith, your lady would like to see you. It's the room below this—did Torquil show you?"

Ferelith nodded and slipped out. When she had gone, Herrian sat in the room's one chair.

"Now, Cradoc. My lady tells me you have a letter for me, from Father Huon?"

"Yes, my lord."

"I've heard a great deal of him," Herrian went on, as Cradoc got out the letter. "In fact, I remember meeting him once, as a boy—he studied for many years on Centre, you know."

Cradoc had not known. He found it hard to imagine Father Huon anywhere but on the edge of the forest on Barren. And he felt a little ashamed of being surprised that Herrian had heard of him and spoke of him with such respect.

Herrian read the letter in silence, and then read it again. Then he looked up.

"The book?"

Cradoc extracted it and gave it to him. The silence lengthened. Cradoc could hear birds singing outside. At last Herrian looked up again.

"This is indeed a great treasure."

As soon as he spoke, Cradoc knew that Torquil had been lying or deceiving himself when he said that Herrian did not believe. A wave of relief swept over him. Herrian was too preoccupied to notice.

"It must go to the archpriest of Lindor," he said, and explained, "This is Lindor, this city, my domain. But when? . . . Tomorrow the archpriest marries me to my lady." A faint smile drifted across his face. "There will be no time. And to delay longer—I shall not rest easy until this is in safekeeping."

He got to his feet, and handed the book back to Cradoc.

"You must take it to him now," he decided. "I shall write a note to go with it and send a servant to show you the way. But do not tell him what you carry. Come."

Less than half an hour later, Cradoc was following Herrian's servant through the streets of Lindor. He carried the book, this time encased in a casket of polished wood. The servant was an old man, and the pace was slow enough for Cradoc to look around him. He was surprised, not by the difference of Centre from Barren, but by the similarity. Of course it was more prosperous, and brighter; the sun was warmer; the buildings were generally white, not gray. But there were the same shops and inns that he had seen on his way to Rya's home, the same street peddlers selling much the same kind of goods. There was no sign that these people had the power to send the silver ships through the air.

At last the servant came to a stop outside a low white house, and pulled a chain outside the door. A deep-toned bell sounded inside. Seconds later the door opened.

"A gift for the archpriest from my lord Herrian."

They were both allowed to pass inside, but the servant remained in the entrance hall, while Cradoc was led further in. After a few moments he was bewildered by the succession of steps and passages; the house must be very old, he guessed, or had had parts added to it later, and he was glad that he had someone to show him the way.

Eventually the archpriest's servant stopped outside a door, knocked and withdrew. Cradoc realized he was alone. Then the door opened and he found himself in the presence of an old man with white hair and a thin, ascetic face. He wore a plain black robe.

"My lord," Cradoc stammered, "I have brought you a gift from my lord Herrian."

"Indeed. Come, then."

His voice was curiously soft. He ushered Cradoc into the room and then left him standing while he looked first at Father Huon's letter, enclosed with a note from Herrian, and then the book itself.

Cradoc shifted from one foot to the other, and passed the time by looking around the room. It was as plain as Father Huon's hut on Barren, although even Cradoc could realize that greater wealth, and greater care, had gone into it. A wooden cross stood on a mantel above a large but empty fireplace. Before the fire was a wooden settle, with no cushions, and a carved wooden chair. The only other furnishings were a table and chair where, from the spread of papers, the archpriest had been working.

At last the archpriest looked up and spoke, in almost the same words that Herrian had used.

"You have brought me a great treasure. And you found it, you say?"

"Yes, my lord."

"And on Barren. Strange." He returned the book to its casket and closed the lid with a click. "Very well. Thank Lord Herrian for his gift, and thank you, too, for your efforts. Tell him we shall speak together of this. You may go."

CHAPTER 9

Cradoc was outside the door before he realized the archpriest had not called the servant to show him the way out. Nothing would have made him go back. He was too insignificant to cause trouble. And besides, something about that austere face and the soft, sibilant voice had frightened him. So he began to try to find his own way back to the entrance.

Soon he had to admit that he was hopelessly lost. He could not find the entrance and he could see no one he could ask. Nervously he began tapping on doors and opening them to see if anyone was there to give him directions. The first he tried was a storeroom, the second led to a cellar stair, and the third led him out into the garden.

He could not resist stepping out into it, marveling at the cool grass and trees, and the brilliant flowers. Somewhere he could hear a trickle of water. Surely no one would be angry to find him here? It was better than wandering around the house, and he might find someone to ask. For a while he followed the crisscrossing paths, disturbing nothing alive except a flight of large, pale butterflies, and then suddenly he realized that he was outside the window of the archpriest's room.

He stepped back, terrified of being seen. Inside the room, he could see the archpriest, pacing restlessly to and fro. After a few moments he came to the window, and stood staring out. Cradoc's heart lurched, but the old man was not looking at him. He seemed not to be looking at anything. His eyes glittered strangely and he kept passing his tongue over his lips. Without knowing why, Cradoc felt chilled. Then the archpriest turned away. Cradoc heard him strike a bell, and a moment later a servant entered the room.

"Have a fire lit here," the archpriest instructed. "Call me when it is burning well."

The servant went out, and the archpriest followed him and closed the door behind him.

10

For a few seconds, Cradoc could not move. What he had just witnessed kept racing through his mind. The archpriest's strange look; the request for a fire on a day as hot as this; the uneasy pacing of the room. He knew what was going to happen. And as soon as he had it straight in his own mind, he was capable of action again.

He slid forward until he stood outside the window. The room was empty. The casket stood on the table. Cradoc knew he had not much time. Soon the servant would return with materials for the fire. Yet he was appalled at what he was about to do. If he were caught in that room, there would be no excuse. No one would believe him. Briefly he hesitated. Was it really possible that the archpriest of Lindor would burn the Word of God?

Somewhere, just on the edge of sight, there was a flicker of golden wings. Cradoc whipped around. He could see nothing but the garden. But he caught a ghost of the fragrance that had filled the air in the forest on Barren, and in his mind there was a voice: "Cradoc—now!" He scrambled over the window sill and dived for the casket. Then, to put off discovery, he took the few extra seconds to open it and take out the book. As he made for the window again he heard the door begin to open. He went out head first and lay flat on the earth below the window with the book clutched to his chest. Then, as soon as he heard the sounds of the fire being set, he began worming his way along the ground until he reached the shelter of some shrubs.

All he had to do now was get away. Nothing would have made him enter that house again. He moved stealthily through the garden, this time hoping he would not encounter anyone. He crawled until he came to a high wall with several trees growing close to it. Tree climbing was something in which he had experience. Thrusting the book down the front of his tunic, he swarmed up the nearest tree and dropped neatly into the street on the other side.

It was a back street, and as far as he could see, deserted. So far, so good. But what was he to do now? If he returned the book to Lord Herrian, he might send it immediately back to the archpriest, for he would surely never believe that he meant to burn it. But Cradoc knew that if he kept it hidden he would have to find a printing press by himself and arrange for the work to be done. Thankfully he thought of Ferelith. She would know what was best. Leaving the book hidden down his tunic, he set off.

Night was falling by the time he walked through the gates into the courtyard. Now it was in uproar. Travelers were streaming through the gates—guests for the wedding, Cradoc supposed—and it was easy for him to slip in unobserved. To his relief, Ferelith was in her room, unpacking. She stopped short at the sight of him.

"Cradoc! What have you—you're filthy, and your tunic's torn. What happened?"

Wordlessly Cradoc held out the book.

"But you took that—tell me what happened."

He told her, as quickly as he could. She listened, horrified, but at least she believed him.

"Give me the book," she said. "Now, go and change. If he sends for you, you must be presentable. Don't argue, just go."

When he returned a few minutes later, the book was nowhere to be seen. Ferelith gave him a smug smile.

"Don't worry, it's safe," she assured him. "And if Herrian asks you, you can say you haven't got it and you don't know where it is."

"But what shall I tell him?" Cradoc asked.

"No more than you have to—at least until you see how he takes it, and what story the archpriest is telling. Remember, he's in a difficult position too. If he gets it back, and then it disappears, Lord Herrian will be very suspicious."

"I wish you could explain to him," Cradoc said despairingly.

"Well, I can't. You'll have to handle it." She sighed heavily. "And we've still got Torquil to worry about. Don't forget about that."

It was after supper before Lord Herrian sent for Cradoc. They met at a veranda overlooking his gardens. He looked tired and harassed.

"Cradoc, I hear a very strange story from the archpriest. He tells me that the book I sent him was heretical."

"My lord?" Cradoc inquired. The word was unfamiliar.

"He means that it told lies about our faith. That it was not the true Word of God at all. So he thought it best to destroy it. However, before he could do so, the book disappeared."

He paused as if expecting a comment, but Cradoc was silent for a moment, admiring the archpriest's cleverness. If he could not destroy the book, discrediting it was just as good—better, perhaps, for he could rely on others trying to destroy it.

"He tells me," Herrian went on, "that you are the only person who could have taken it. Is that true?"

Cradoc hesitated, swallowed, and decided on the truth.

"Yes, my lord."

He explained how he had come to be in the garden and what he had seen there. Herrian listened in silence. When Cradoc had finished, he drew a long breath, thrusting his hands through his hair.

"You give me a problem, Cradoc," he said. "All this, now . . . with the wedding tomorrow. . . . The book is safe?"

"Yes, my lord." Tentatively, he added, "You believe me?"

Herrian smiled wearily.

"Oh, yes. I believe you. You see, I know the archpriest. He is an old man, perhaps overfond of his own authority and afraid of change. And what you carry, Cradoc, seems set to change us all. We have built our lives on men's memories of what God told us. Now that we can read His own words, we're bound to find that many things we believed were wrong or mistaken, and that many things were forgotten. It will take courage to reorder things as they should be. Besides—I was convinced in a few minutes that this book is the true Word of God. I believe it would take a study of many months, perhaps years, to prove that it is not."

He paced the length of the veranda and back, and leaned on the rail looking out over the garden.

"I expected that the archpriest would arrange for the printing of the book," he said. "Perhaps I should have foreseen what he would do. He has declared the book heretical, which means we can expect no help from the church here. Perhaps not in other places either if he sends word to other cities. We must arrange for the printing ourselves. The truth cannot be denied forever. Cradoc, are you willing to go on a journey?"

He did not wait for Cradoc's reply. In any case, his sudden alert look was answer enough.

"There is no printing press in Lindor," he explained. "There was one once, but accidents were always happening—spilled ink, damaged machinery, mysterious fires. . . ."

He gave Cradoc a quizzical look to see if he had got the point.

"Someone was causing it?" Cradoc asked.

"Someone was—and I know who. South of here, Cradoc, is a greater city than this—Andarre, domain of the Lord Baric. He's here now for the wedding. He's a harsh man, an enemy to learning and to the church. He permits no church in Andarre and he would destroy it everywhere else. Our printing press was too useful to the church, and so . . . In the end, we grew tired of so many accidents. We announced that the press was closing down. But in fact, we moved it."

"Where?"

Herrian gave him a mischievous grin.

"We moved it to Andarre. We smuggled in the machinery. Now we smuggle in paper and smuggle out books. It's the last place Baric would think to look. My master printer organizes it all. We call him the Mouse."

"The Mouse?"

"There's a proverb on Centre—it's an unquiet mouse that sleeps in a cat's ear. He's an unquiet mouse in Andarre, and a brave man. And in a few days, Cradoc, I shall send you to him.

When the wedding is over and the guests disperse, you shall go too, quietly. There may be danger. Are you ready for that?"

"Oh, yes, my lord!"

Herrian sighed.

"I wish I had your certainty, Cradoc," he said. "I don't think you know what you're carrying or what upheaval it's going to cause. On Centre we do what we can. I think I fear your new world almost as much as the archpriest does. Don't they hate us on Barren?" he went on, as if he were changing the subject. "Don't they see us as wealthy and powerful, and refusing to share what we have?"

Cradoc murmured something, remembering his last conversation with the overseer.

"Yet we're not so very different," Herrian went on. "Oh, Lindor is prosperous, but there are places on Centre just as poor as anywhere on Barren. But all through the years we have clung to the secret of space travel because if we could not send the ships, the Six Worlds would lose contact with each other and slide back into barbarism. So we build fires of wood and make our journeys on horseback and save what fuel we have for the ships and the radios that speak from world to world."

His hands clenched as if in frustration.

"We have so few resources, Cradoc, so few trained men. Each year we gain a little ground, but it takes so long and it could be snuffed out so easily. And I ask myself, Cradoc, will your discovery renew us, or will it shatter the little we have achieved? I can only go on, and trust in God."

He laid a hand on Cradoc's shoulder, smiling. Cradoc felt the sudden sting of tears and was glad he had been honest with this man.

"I'll send for you again soon," Herrian told him. "And I'll do what I can to make sure you have a safe journey. And Cradoc," he added, as the boy turned to go, "we haven't had this conversation."

11

On the following evening, Cradoc hovered near the doors of the great hall, watching the guests going in to dinner. That morning Lord Herrian had married Lady Rya and it looked as if half the nobility of Centre had come to see and to celebrate. Cradoc was intrigued to see so many different people, all so unlike what he was used to. But he did not watch with the wonder he would have felt not very long ago. He was growing more experienced.

He moved a hand to feel the shape of the book. Ferelith had returned it to him and had sewn a kind of pocket inside his tunic so he could always carry it. The responsibility of keeping it safe until he could start for Andarre weighed heavily on him. He hoped it would be over soon.

A hand plucked at his sleeve. It was Ferelith.

"Follow me," she said, beckoning.

She led the way up a narrow staircase and out onto a section of gallery overlooking the great hall. Another section of it was occupied by musicians, but otherwise it was deserted. There were chairs and a table that had been laid with an inviting supper.

"I had a word with one of my lady's servants," Ferelith explained, her eyes dancing. "We can sit up here and see everything that's going on. And I expect we'll have more fun than they will down there."

Cradoc joined her, smiling. They sat by the gallery rail watching the guests take their places. At last music sounded and Lord Herrian and Lady Rya appeared on the high table. The dinner began. Cradoc and Ferelith shared their supper and shared their surprise at some of the strange dishes that were brought in down below. There was a whole swan roasted in its feathers, pies in fanciful shapes, and other things that not even Ferelith could put a name to.

"I wish we knew who all these people are," she said. "I feel I'd like to know some of them. And some of them I'm very glad I don't know!"

"There's one you know, anyway," Cradoc remarked.

He pointed to where Torquil was making his way down the hall, more richly dressed than before in a tunic of dark blue silk, edged with gold. He was carrying a harp.

"I forgot. He said he was my lord's harper."

"Then let's hope he's been so busy practicing his piece," Ferelith said acidly, "that he hasn't had time to think about the book." She giggled. "Perhaps he'll sound like cats on a roof!"

Torquil spoke briefly to Lord Herrian and then settled himself to play in a space in the middle of the hall. From the first notes, Cradoc forgot his quarrel with the harper. He had never heard music before except for songs sung in chorus on the farm. And he had never imagined that sound could be as beautiful as this. Ferelith was listening, enraptured, all her mockery abandoned. For a while there was nothing except the soaring voice and the cascading notes of the harp. Cradoc did not know how long it lasted. There was time for quiet songs to succeed lively ones, for brilliant instrumental pieces that seemed designed to demonstrate the player's skill, and simple, poignant tunes that brought a lump to Cradoc's throat. And at last it was over.

Torquil bowed to Lord Herrian and to Rya and began to withdraw. Conversation that had died as he played started up again. Several of the guests called to Torquil, seeming to congratulate him on his performance, so his progress toward the doors of the hall was slow. He had little to say to anyone, except that Cradoc noticed he spoke for some time to a tall man dressed entirely in black, seated about halfway down the hall. Then that conversation was interrupted by another guest, drunk and enthusiastic, who tried to give Torquil a cup of wine. When Torquil refused, the man thrust it at him so that the wine spilt over Torquil's tunic. At that Torquil excused himself and made more rapidly for the door.

Cradoc watched all this with interest and suddenly got to his feet.

"Just a minute," he said to Ferelith.

He returned down the staircase and found Torquil just outside the doors to the hall. One arm cradled his harp, while the other hand scrubbed at the wine stains on his tunic. Cradoc spoke his name. Torquil looked up, startled.

"Oh—good evening, Cradoc Birdscarer." There was no sarcasm in his voice.

"We heard your music," Cradoc said. "It was beautiful."

Torquil gave him a long look out of wide, dark eyes.

"Thank you."

Cradoc had meant to say no more than that. He would have felt somehow humiliated if his dislike of Torquil had prevented him from saying how much the music had meant to him. But another impulse followed the first, and he went on. "Have you had any supper? Do you want to come and share ours?"

Now the harper looked definitely surprised.

"No, I—" He stopped. "Very well, if you wish. But I am not very good company after I have played."

Cradoc resisted the temptation to say he had not been very good company beforehand, either. He waited while Torquil collected the case for his harp from a bench by the outer door. Then he led him up the stairs. When they appeared, Ferelith shot him a glance of surprise and disapproval but said nothing. Cradoc found a seat for Torquil and offered him some food, but the harper refused nearly everything. Cradoc realized he was exhausted. And more than that—the performance had drained everything out of him. He did not even have the energy to be malicious.

After a while, at Cradoc's request, he began telling them the names of some of the guests and a little about them. Ferelith grew interested, and Cradoc hoped she had forgiven him.

"Which is Lord Baric?" he asked, trying to sound casual.

"There, on the high table, next to my Lord Herrian."

The man Torquil pointed out looked to be in his fifties, broad and fleshy, gazing about him with a magisterial air. Cradoc disliked him on sight.

"What have you to do with Lord Baric?" Torquil asked.

"Nothing. I just heard the name."

"Well, he's heard yours. Or at least he's heard of you. I was speaking to his Master of Horse—the man in black there, halfway down that table. He'd got some sort of story from the archpriest's household about a heretical book that some boy had brought from Barren."

"Torquil!" Ferelith exclaimed.

"What did you say?" Cradoc asked tensely.

"I told him I'd seen the book—but of course, I cannot judge whether it is heretical or not. He asked if you were still in the court. When I said you were, he wanted me to bring you to see his lord later tonight. Of course, I said I could not do so without my lord Herrian's consent."

Cradoc and Ferelith exchanged despairing glances. Cradoc supposed he should have expected the archpriest's household to set rumors flying, but it was his own fault that Torquil was able to confirm them.

"We must tell Lord Herrian!" he exclaimed.

"Lord Herrian is otherwise occupied," the harper pointed out. "I dare say he will receive you some time tomorrow."

"Tomorrow will be too late," Cradoc said impatiently. "Ferelith, what shall we do?"

"I'll write him a note. Perhaps one of the servants will take it in to him." She looked around her. "There's nothing to write it on here. You'll have to wait."

She disappeared rapidly down the stairs. Cradoc turned to the harper.

"I told you it was supposed to be secret!"

Torquil shrugged.

"It isn't secret any longer."

"You didn't have to gossip about it!"

"He asked; I answered. I told him nothing he didn't know already."

Cradoc wondered about that, but he said no more. They waited in silence until Ferelith returned.

"I've done it," she said. "Now we'll see."

They watched the hall below and in a few moments a servant approached Lord Herrian and handed him something. Herrian studied it. At first they thought he would do nothing, but then he rose, excused himself to Rya and the guests around him, and left the hall. When he appeared at the top of the stairs, he looked annoyed.

"Cradoc—what is this? I hope you have a good explanation. Torquil, Ferelith, you'd better go."

Torquil had risen when his lord entered and was moving to obey. But Ferelith stood her ground.

"My lord, Torquil and I both know about the book. I think we should stay."

Herrian stared at her. Cradoc saw his sudden tension and realized he was frightened.

"Rya?" he asked.

"No, my lord. She knows nothing."

Herrian seemed to relax a little and moved further into the gallery.

"Cradoc," he began, his voice icy, "I thought you understood your mission was secret."

Cradoc straightened and forced himself to meet Herrian's eyes.

"Yes, my lord, I know. It was my fault."

"I can excuse your inexperience, Cradoc, but not sheer stupidity. And now Baric knows. Would you care to explain that?"

Rapidly Cradoc related what Torquil had told them. Herrian turned his attention to the harper who was standing white and rigid.

"Torquil, there is little excuse for you. You know Baric. You know what he will do with this information."

"My lord, I—"

"Be quiet. All I can do now is think what we might do to mend matters."

He hesitated and went on, "Baric is fully occupied for some time yet. His man cannot speak to him until this dinner is over. You have a little time. What you must do, all of you, is to leave the court now. Disappear before Baric can lay hands on you. And since you must go somewhere, you may as well take the book to Andarre. Though I must be mad to entrust it to such careless guardians."

"Now?" Cradoc asked.

"My lord—" Torquil began to protest.

"Silence!" Herrian's voice was quiet, but it held the lash of anger. "I will assume your fault was indiscretion rather than actual treachery. But you will do as I say. You are no longer safe in the court."

"But I know nothing, my lord!"

"You have seen the book and you know what it is, which is more than Baric knows at present. And you can lead him to Cradoc. A talk with you is exactly what Baric will want. And I doubt you could keep silence if he became persistent."

Torquil's face flamed, but he said no more. Herrian turned back to Cradoc.

"When I say you must go now, I mean exactly that. There's no time to prepare you, but you have yourselves to thank for that. The one consolation is that the last place that Baric will expect you to make for is Andarre. But the main roads will not be safe. Listen carefully. Go out of Lindor by the South Gate—Torquil will show you the way—and take the road south. After about a mile, a track goes off to the left through a grove of trees. Take that track. It leads up into the hills and through a pass, and from there down into the plains and at last to Andarre. Travel by night and rest concealed by day. That way you may avoid Baric's men. You have the book?"

"Yes, my lord."

Herrian looked at Ferelith who had quietly begun collecting the remains of the supper—bread, cold meat and fruit, into napkins.

"I'm sorry, Ferelith," he said. "You seem to be innocent in all this, but you are not safe here now and so you must go. I'll explain as best I can to your lady."

"Thank you, my lord," she said, and added daringly, "I'm glad I'm to go. Someone has to keep them out of trouble."

Herrian smiled reluctantly.

"I hope you can do it. Here—I haven't much money about me, but take this, such as it is. It will buy food for the journey. You can expect to be on the road for five, perhaps six nights."

"And when we reach Andarre, my lord?" Cradoc asked.

"I'll send word to the Mouse. He'll expect you. Now you must go and I must return to the dinner before Baric wonders where I've gone."

He motioned to them to go down the stairs before him. Torquil, by now unable to conceal his distress, made one more protest.

"My lord—to travel on foot to Andarre, by night—I can't!"

"Why not? It will do you good."

Herrian's tone was scathing, but then he softened slightly.

"Don't worry, Torquil, I will receive you again when this is all over. I hope by then you will have learned discretion."

The harper followed Cradoc and Ferelith without another word, and Lord Herrian went back to the hall.

12

As he began the journey, Cradoc could not help feeling optimistic in spite of all that had happened and the danger they were now in. At least he was on the way to Andarre where the book would be printed, and finally safe. Beside him, Ferelith was swinging her bundle jauntily.

"It's a fine night for a walk," she remarked.

"You might not think that when you've walked as far as Andarre," Cradoc replied. "I'm sorry, Ferelith. You could have stayed with your lady if I hadn't been so stupid."

"Oh, I see! You thought you could sneak off without me, did you? I've already said I want to come."

"I'm sorry about Torquil, too," Cradoc added in a lower voice.

The harper, still carrying his instrument, was walking just ahead of them and leading the way to the South Gate. He had not spoken since they left the hall.

"He asked for it," Ferelith said. "Lord Herrian was right. It will do him good. I'm sorry we have to put up with him, though."

Cradoc said no more, but his conscience was not quiet. If he had kept his temper, Torquil would have known nothing and would have been spared this journey and his lord's anger.

It was growing late, but there was still a little light in the summer sky when they reached the South Gate. Cradoc had wondered if the gate would be guarded, but people were still passing to and fro through it.

There were huts and cottages built outside the walls, and it looked as if the people who lived there were celebrating Lord Herrian's wedding. At any rate, the road outside was crowded enough that no one was likely to have noticed their departure.

They found the track Lord Herrian had spoken of without trouble and struck off into the trees. The trees had an invigorating, spicy smell. It was cool and the leaves rustled in a faint breeze. At a distance, Cradoc could hear the barking of a dog. Everything was very peaceful. Cradoc found it hard to believe that soon he might have an enemy on his trail.

"Have you been this way before, Torquil?" he asked.

He thought the harper was not going to reply, but eventually he said, "No," in an icy voice that discouraged Cradoc from trying to talk to him. Ferelith chattered away easily, pointing out this and that. Cradoc answered her, but he could not quite forget the silent presence of the harper.

After a while the track began to climb. Trees gave way to upland meadows, fragrant with flowers. It was fully dark now. Centre's two small moons were in the sky and gave enough light to walk by. The city fell away behind them. They might have been in an empty world. Hours passed. Even Ferelith grew silent at last. Cradoc wondered about his companions' powers of endurance. He was used to hard work and little food, and little sleep either, if there was work to be done. The journey to Andarre presented no problems for him. But he knew he could not expect Ferelith or Torquil to match him in strength.

They kept going, however, until the path grew steeper still, doubling back and forth across the hillside. The grass here was shorter and tougher. Great outcrops of rock thrust through the thin soil. Cradoc lifted his head and saw the line of the hills above them, dipping down at one point to what might be the pass. They would not reach it that night. He decided they ought to start looking for a sheltered spot to rest that would be concealed from anyone who might be following.

Among the rocks he hoped to find what he wanted. He had not done so yet when Torquil sank down at the side of the path and said, "You go on; I can't."

"Don't be stupid!" Ferelith exclaimed.

Cradoc shook his head at her.

"We can't do that," he said quietly. "What would you do, out here? We'll stop in a few minutes as soon as we find somewhere safe. Come on. I'll help you. Shall I carry the harp?"

He put a hand on Torquil's shoulder as he spoke. The harper shook him off savagely.

"Leave me alone!"

He got to his feet and trudged on up the path. Cradoc and Ferelith followed.

The last half hour was the most difficult. In some places they really needed to climb, and Torquil, encumbered by the harp, found it almost impossible. Cradoc listened to his sobbing breath and thought of how his first offer of help had been received, so he said nothing. He was relieved when he found the perfect place for their camp—a narrow ravine winding away from the path. Around a shoulder of rock they were concealed from everything except the sky above. The stars were already paling toward dawn.

"There's even water!" Ferelith said with satisfaction, kneeling beside the trickle and splashing her face. "Oh, that's good! Come along, then—breakfast is served."

She opened her bundle and portioned out bread and cold meat for the three of them. Cradoc sat beside her. Torquil was huddled on the ground a short ways off.

"Torquil—breakfast," Ferelith said imperiously.

"I don't want it."

"Don't talk nonsense!" She ignored Cradoc's attempt to interrupt. "Personally, Torquil, I don't care whether you eat or not. But somehow we've got to get to Andarre, and if you faint with hunger, there's nothing we can do for you up here."

Before she had finished speaking, Torquil had dragged himself to his feet and approached her. As she handed him the food, she added, "If you're going to behave like this, we'll all be raving lunatics long before we get to Andarre."

"Leave me alone!" Torquil retorted. "If it weren't for you, I wouldn't be here."

"And if you hadn't—"

"No, stop it," Cradoc interrupted. "You're right, Torquil, and I'm sorry. But we're here now and there's nothing we can do about it. It's not so bad, really."

Torquil said nothing and withdrew a few paces to eat in silence. He sat with head bowed, looking utterly defeated. Cradoc felt his dislike dissolving into pity, but he did not know what to do about it. He knew Torquil would reject any attempt at friendliness as fiercely as he had rejected help on the road.

By the time their meal was finished it was almost full light, but in their hiding place the rocks cast deep shadows from the rising sun they could not see. Cradoc leaned back against the rock.

"I don't feel like sleep," he said. "Torquil, will you play for us?"

The harper looked up at him, no longer hostile. His expression was unreadable.

"No," he said shortly.

"Perhaps you're right," Cradoc replied. "We ought to keep quiet"—though he did not think Torquil had refused for that reason. Instead, he brought out the book.

"Read to us, Ferelith."

Ferelith took the book and opened it. Her face grew intent. She began to read quietly.

"When you pass through deep waters, I am with you. When you pass through rivers, they will not sweep you away. Walk through fire and you will not be scorched, through flames and they will not burn you."

Cradoc listened and found peace and reassurance spreading through him. His hand sought Father Huon's wooden cross hidden beneath his tunic. They were not alone. With courage and resolution they could fulfill their task. He wanted to share his conviction with the harper, but Torquil had turned away and was sleeping, or at least pretending. At last Ferelith put the book aside.

"I'm tired, Cradoc."

He smiled at her and she curled up neatly and closed her eyes. Cradoc wondered if someone ought to keep watch, but he was tired too, and the day was growing warm. While he was still considering the question, he too fell asleep.

13

Cradoc woke with a start and sat up. At first he thought he had not slept long, for shadows still stretched across the ravine. Then he realized the shadows stretched the other way. The sun was setting. He looked around. Torquil still lay in the same position. Ferelith was up, washing at the tiny stream. Cradoc joined her and splashed the cold water over his face and neck.

"I was going to wake you," she said. "We'll be able to start soon. Do you want something to eat?"

"Should we?"

"We can have a bite now, and that will leave something for our next stop. After that . . ." she sighed. "Lord Herrian did give us some money. There must be somewhere we can buy food. Or we could try living off the country. Did you ever catch rabbits on Barren, Cradoc Birdscarer?"

Cradoc grinned at her.

"Yes. You need a snare and a lot of time and patience."

Ferelith shrugged and went to where she had left the provisions.

"Oh, my feet ache," she complained. "I wish Herrian had thought to give us horses."

"You couldn't get horses up here," Cradoc reminded her. "Or hide them very easily."

"I know, I know." She began dividing up the food. "Go and wake Torquil, will you?"

Cradoc crossed the ravine to where Torquil was lying. The harper sat up as he approached. Cradoc wondered how long he had been awake.

"How do you feel?" he asked.

"I'm all right."

The brusque response did not invite any more conversation, but at least he ate his share of the food and got ready to start the journey without any protest. At dusk, they moved off again.

They reached the pass by about midnight. By this time both Torquil and Ferelith were finding the going difficult. Both were wearing soft leather slippers which had been suitable for an evening in the court, but not for traveling over rough country. Cradoc, who was used to going barefoot, offered his boots to either of them, but met with two refusals along with an acid comment from Ferelith about the size of his feet.

There was a cold wind at this height, too, and even Cradoc found himself wishing now and again for a cloak or a vest. Their journey no longer seemed so pleasant. Compared with the night before, they covered very little ground, mostly scrambling and climbing among rocks. Even Torquil had to accept help at last, if only to hand the harp to one of the others to leave both hands free to climb. However, Cradoc was reasonably satisfied when they reached the pass with half the night still ahead.

They stopped for a brief rest and looked at the country spread before them. Moonlight showed them the same rocky landscape, giving way at last to grassland and then to some kind of massed foliage that Cradoc could not identify. In the valley there was the glint of a river.

"That's the boundary of my lord Herrian's lands," Torquil volunteered.

Cradoc was surprised. It was about the first time he had spoken without being spoken to.

"Is there a bridge, do you know?" he asked.

"I'm not sure. I think so."

Beyond the river the land faded into darkness. Cradoc was sure they would not be able to see Andarre from this distance, even in daylight.

"Time we moved on," he said.

"Slave driver," Ferelith remarked, without malice.

They moved on. As Cradoc had expected, going down was much more difficult than going up. It was so much easier to make a false step. To add to their problems, there were clouds coming up that obscured the moons from time to time. Sometimes it grew so dark that they could do nothing but wait for it to clear again. Even a slight injury would have been serious out there.

By the end of the night even Cradoc was exhausted. They seemed to have been struggling among the rocks for days without number. At last, with relief, he discerned the approach of dawn and began to think about finding a place to stop.

"And about time, too!" Ferelith said, looking as if she would say more once she had the energy.

Cradoc went on to the next turn in the path. He could see no obvious refuge like the one they had found the night before. A sharp cry behind him made him turn. Torquil had missed his footing and had fallen awkwardly, trying to save the harp. When Cradoc reached him he was sitting up, rubbing his wrist and flexing the fingers of his hand. He looked close to tears.

"What's the matter? Are you hurt?" Cradoc asked.

The harper seemed to recover as he spoke.

"No—no, it's all right," he said. He seemed to think he had to explain, for he added, "I was afraid—I'm always afraid of hurting my hands—because of the music."

Cradoc half smiled.

"I see. Come on, then. It's not far now."

He helped Torquil to his feet. For a change the harper did not protest. Cradoc could not miss the slight gasp of pain as Torquil put his weight on his right foot.

"You are hurt!" he said.

"No, it's nothing. I can walk on it."

He started off, demonstrating that he could, though his mouth was set with pain. Cradoc and Ferelith followed a pace behind. Fortunately the path was leveling out. They had almost reached the grassland.

"He's not going to keep going," Cradoc murmured to Ferelith. "Not as far as Andarre."

"He'll have to."

Cradoc shook his head uneasily. His fears increased when he saw Torquil stop suddenly, but then, drawing level with him, he realized why. Below them, beyond the next few twists and turns of the path, was a building, or a group of buildings, huddled together in the sheltered side of the rocks at the very edge of the pasture. Sound was already rising from it—a dog barking, very faintly, the sound of someone whistling. A herd of goats and their keeper appeared from the far side and straggled off into the fields. Cradoc had a sudden pang of homesickness.

"A farm," Ferelith said. "What do you think?"

He looked at her questioningly.

"We could stay there, perhaps," she suggested.

Cradoc was not so sure. "Is it safe?"

"We're still in Herrian's lands. And it's remote enough. They might let us stay. We've money and could pay them. At the very least we could buy food. We must buy food, Cradoc, there's practically nothing left."

Cradoc nodded.

"What do you think, Torquil?"

The harper looked surprised to be consulted.

"I don't know. It's up to you."

Cradoc considered. Ferelith, for all her courage, looked really exhausted—almost as bad as Torquil, though she concealed it better. And Cradoc was seriously worried about the harper. A day's real rest, perhaps with a fire and hot food, and the chance to see to his injured foot might make all the difference. Straightening, he made his decision.

"All right," he said. "The farm it is."

14

As they entered the farmyard, a dog began barking eagerly at the end of its rope. A woman appeared in the doorway of the house. She was tall and dark, with a formidable expression that dissolved into concern when she saw the state they were in. Cradoc began to explain, but she did not let him get very far.

"Traveling by night, indeed! You look like it, you poor, silly creatures. Come into the kitchen."

"We can pay for food and lodging," Ferelith told her as they followed her. "Or perhaps there's work we could do to help you?"

"Work? You look fit for nothing but to drop in your tracks. You're going to eat and sleep, and maybe we'll talk about payment afterward."

Even Cradoc was too tired to protest. They sat at the large, scrubbed table in the kitchen and ate porridge from a steaming pot on the fire. As they drank some fresh milk they told the woman, whose name, she said, was Hild, what they could about their journey. Cradoc did not divulge the reason for their journey, not because he felt he could not trust the woman, but because she might at some time be questioned. Ferelith, to his relief, followed his lead. Torquil was too absorbed in fighting sleep to talk at all. Cradoc thought Hild was shrewd enough to realize they were keeping something back, but she asked no awkward questions. When she learned they came from Lindor, she asked about Lord Herrian's marriage and what Lady Rya was like. That topic got them safely through the meal.

By the time it was over, Torquil had given up the struggle and was asleep at the table with his head pillowed on his arms. Hild half-lifted him and guided him over to a wooden bench by the kitchen fire. He curled up there apparently without having woken at all.

"He can stay there," Hild said. "As for you two, can you sleep in the hayloft? It's dry and clean, and you'll be no trouble."

Cradoc and Ferelith thanked her. Hild led them out into the yard again. The hayloft was reached by a short wooden ladder and was piled high with sweet-smelling bundles of hay. The only other occupants were a cat and four kittens. Cradoc arranged beds for himself and Ferelith. It was not long before they followed Torquil into sleep.

Hours later Cradoc woke with the sensation that something was wrong. He sat up and looked around. Ferelith still slept nearby. Sunlight slanted in through the tiny window. Everything seemed peaceful. Then he heard again the sound that had woken him. Looking out of the window, he saw three horses in the yard. Quickly he roused Ferelith.

"Horses in the yard?" she murmured, still half asleep. "Of course there are horses in the yard. This is a farm."

"They aren't farm horses."

Reluctantly she dragged herself to her feet and looked out of the window. The last traces of her sleep vanished.

"No, they're not."

Cradoc turned as he heard a voice calling them from the bottom of the ladder. It was Hild.

"Three men, and I don't like the look of them," she said as they joined her. "Turned me out of my own kitchen! They're in there now, talking to your friend."

Cradoc and Ferelith exchanged a glance of dismay.

"Is there anywhere we can hear what they're saying?" Cradoc asked.

"Outside the window, if you want to risk it." She led the way, giving Cradoc a grim smile. "You know who they are, don't you? I thought there was something you didn't tell me."

She pointed out the window of the kitchen and went back into the house. Cradoc and Ferelith approached cautiously.

"Keep a lookout," Cradoc instructed in a whisper. "One of them might come out."

CHAPTER 14

He edged closer to the window. In the section of the room that he could see, one man was lounging on the bench near the fire. A second stood with his back to Cradoc, blocking out the rest of the room. Cradoc could hear movement that suggested the third man was still in there. The two he could see were wearing plain, dark tunics, not uniforms. Baric, he supposed, would not like to reveal that his men were here in Herrian's lands. Cradoc had no doubt at all that that was who they were.

The first thing he heard was Torquil's voice, sounding as languid and superior as it had on their first meeting.

"I have already told you, I am my lord Herrian's harper, from Lindor."

Cradoc could not see him or guess what he would say. He wanted to trust him, but he was afraid he could not.

"And what is my lord Herrian's harper from Lindor doing here?"

"I had a fancy to travel. Harpers frequently do."

"Don't try to be clever with me. Your sort don't travel, not by that road and not alone. Or perhaps you aren't alone? What about the boy from Barren?"

"I hope you don't think I'm in the habit of associating with a farm boy from Barren?"

Cradoc could not suppress a faint smile. His breath came more easily. At least Torquil intended to lie his way out of trouble.

"But you met this boy, didn't you?"

"Of course I met him. And I found him extremely tedious. I can't imagine why you want to know about him."

"I want to know about the book he was carrying."

"The book? Yes, he was carrying a book."

"Has he still got it?"

"How should I know?"

The man with his back to Cradoc stepped forward. There was the sound of a blow and a gasp of pain from Torquil.

"Now are you going to answer my questions?"

But the voice that replied was as disdainful as ever.

"I have already done so."

Ferelith tugged at Cradoc's arm.

"We've got to get out of here."

"We can't. We can't leave Torquil."

"But the book—"

"I know. But—listen."

The man had moved forward again. Cradoc could see him leaning over the kitchen table where Torquil must have been sitting. He was saying something in a voice too soft for Cradoc to make out the words. But its effect on Torquil was clear enough.

"Oh, no—no!" His composure had crumbled away. His voice was high pitched, pleading. "Not my hands—please, not my hands!"

"In five minutes, lad, I could make sure that you never play that harp again."

Cold horror touched Cradoc. For a few seconds he almost forgot his own danger.

"No—no, don't! I'll tell you everything!"

"Well?"

"He's here, somewhere. We came from Lindor together. He has the book. Lord Herrian made me come—oh, please, please don't!"

There was the sound of another blow and the desperate pleas gave way to violent sobbing. Cradoc had already taken out the book and thrust it at Ferelith.

"Take it, and go."

"I can't."

"You have to. Don't you see, they don't know about you. You can take it to Andarre."

"But you—"

"Never mind me. Oh, Ferelith, don't argue. Just go."

She looked as if she could have argued, but after a second's hesitation she took the book and sped away around the side of the house. Cradoc stood still.

15

Inside the room, the leader was giving orders for a search, and Cradoc heard the other two men leaving. He knew hiding would be no use, but misdirection might, and he might buy time for Ferelith. Returning to the yard, he saw a broom propped against a wall. By the time the men appeared, he was sweeping the stones in a leisurely fashion as if he had nothing more urgent on his mind than his next meal.

At first the men ignored him. One went up into the hayloft and came down again at once, saying to the other, "I reckon he's been sleeping up there."

They both went off toward the stables.

Cradoc went on sweeping. The way to the gate was clear. He could have made a dash for it, but he could not leave Torquil. He pitied the harper deeply and he was afraid of what else he might tell, for he knew now that the men had broken him utterly.

At last the men reappeared.

"Hi! You there!"

Cradoc ignored the call. One of them came and grabbed his shoulder.

"You! Are you deaf?"

Cradoc looked up, his mouth open. Stupidity had been an excellent defense in his days on the farm on Barren.

"Daft, more like," the other said. "Listen, boy." He bent down and spoke very slowly and clearly. "Have you seen a boy here?"

Cradoc grinned and nodded, and pointed toward the house.

"Yes, master. Harper. In there."

"No, not him. Another, with him?"

"Yes, master."

"Where is he now?"

"Gone, master. Two hours ago."

It might have worked. It very nearly did. The two men left him and began to walk toward the house, and then one stopped and turned.

"Wait a minute. This is a boy."

"He's a farm boy."

"It's a farm boy we're looking for. Here—you! Come here."

Cradoc obeyed.

"Maybe I'm stupid," the man said, "but I'd just like the harper to have a look at you. Come on."

Cradoc shrugged and went with them. There was no point in resisting.

Inside the kitchen the leader who had questioned Torquil was pacing restlessly. He was a big man, heavy and brutish, but not, Cradoc thought, unintelligent. He had found Torquil's weak point soon enough. The harper was collapsed over the table, weeping pitifully. Cradoc wondered if he had been questioned any further.

The men escorting him thrust him forward and he stood in front of their leader.

"Is this him?"

"I don't know. He's the only boy we could find."

The leader grabbed Torquil's shoulder and hauled him upright.

"Is this him?" he repeated.

"Yes," Torquil gasped, shrinking away. "Oh, Cradoc, I couldn't help it."

The leader was searching Cradoc efficiently.

"All right, where is it?" he asked. "The book," he added, when Cradoc said nothing.

When Cradoc still said nothing, he turned back to Torquil.

"Well? Where is it?"

"I don't know. No—I promise you—I don't know!"

The leader seemed to believe him. He was shaking with

terror and obviously incapable of concealing anything. Quietly, the leader spoke to Cradoc.

"One of you is going to tell me where the book is. If you don't, your friend here is never going to play the harp again."

He clamped a hand down on Torquil's wrist, pinning it to the table. With the other hand he took out a short, ugly knife. Torquil struggled ineffectually. For a moment his sobs were the only sound in the room. He was gazing at Cradoc despairingly.

"Cradoc, don't let him!" he begged.

Cradoc took a breath.

"It isn't here."

"Then where is it?"

"I don't know."

"That's not good enough."

The hand with the knife moved closer to Torquil's straining fingers.

"What shall I do?" Cradoc's question was unspoken, but directed with a desperate need to that overwhelming presence, the Phoenix who had twice now set him on the path he was to follow. This third time there was no answering flash of gold, only a whimpering sound as the harper crumpled into a faint across the table.

The leader snorted with disgust and released him, sheathing the knife.

"All right," he said to his men. "We'll have to do it the hard way. Start searching. You're looking for a book—you know what a book looks like?"

The men muttered and nodded and left. Cradoc and the leader faced each other.

"So," the leader said. "That little game is over. But once your friend wakes, we can start another. If you won't tell me where the book is, you might like to tell me something else, like where you were taking it."

Cradoc said nothing. There was no point. The leader resumed his pacing. Torquil lay still as death.

A few moments later there was a tap on the door and it opened. Cradoc felt his heart stop. The newcomer was Ferelith—

not guarded, not the disheveled fugitive, but pert and pretty with an apron and a tray with a jar of wine and cups. Her glance flickered over Torquil as if fainting harpers were all part of the day's work and she bobbed a curtsy to the leader.

"A cup of wine, master?"

The leader growled an assent. Ferelith set the tray down and began to pour. The leader turned his back on her in his pacing and instantly she brought the heavy wine jar down on his head. It shattered. There was wine everywhere and the leader slumped heavily to the floor where he lay still.

Ferelith giggled.

"I really enjoyed that," she said.

Cradoc tried to pull himself together.

"I told you to go."

"I did go—as far as the house. I found myself an apron and a job to do. Hild helped. Now stop fussing. We've got to go."

"Not without Torquil."

"Cradoc—he betrayed us."

"And he could tell them more. They don't know about you yet, or the Mouse."

He could not begin to explain his other reasons for wanting to help Torquil. Ferelith murmured something, but went over to Torquil and began shaking him vigorously. After a moment his eyes fluttered open and a moan of terror escaped him.

"Torquil," Cradoc said, "get up—we can go."

The harper obviously did not understand. Cradoc and Ferelith got him to his feet and half-supported him toward the door. Before they reached it, he stopped dead.

"My harp."

"Leave it," Ferelith said. "It's no more than a nuisance."

"No—no, I won't."

To save argument Cradoc fetched it and the harper stood hugging it to him while Ferelith looked out of the door.

"All clear," she reported.

Stealthily they slipped out into the yard. There was no sign of the other men. The gate stood open. Expecting to hear a shout behind them, they crossed the yard, passed the gate, and set off down the track into the valley. There was no sound of pursuit. For the time being they had escaped, but none of them was stupid enough to imagine that the danger was over.

16

Some way down the road, Cradoc stopped and looked back. The farm was out of sight, and everything was quiet.

"They'll start looking for us soon," he said. "We should get off the road."

The hillside offered them no cover, but a little lower down began the massed foliage they had seen from the pass. As they drew nearer, Cradoc realized they were vines, heavy with grapes almost ready for picking. He had never seen them growing before. He remarked as much to Ferelith, who said crossly, "You're not here to study agriculture, Cradoc Birdscarer. We can hide in them. That's all that matters to me."

Crouching, they moved along the green tunnels between the vines until they had put a couple of hundred yards between themselves and the road.

"Let's rest," Cradoc said.

Though they had come such a short way, he felt exhausted. It was the relief from their immediate danger. And already he had to think ahead.

"Ferelith," he said, "you have got the book?"

Ferelith pulled out a couple of cleaning rags from her apron pocket and revealed the book underneath.

"I'm not stupid."

"Then we go on—if we can."

As he spoke they heard the drumming of hoofbeats. Horses—two or perhaps three—swept past them on the road.

"They're looking," Ferelith said softly.

"Then we stay here until nightfall. They might guess we're in hiding, but they can't search the whole vineyard."

By this time it was late afternoon. The sun slanted through the vines creating a dappled green cavern that shut out the rest of the world. Ferelith sat with her chin on her hands, looking moody. Torquil was stretched out on the ground, his face hidden in the crook of one arm. Even in the warm sunlight he was shivering, and Cradoc thought he was silently crying. Cradoc reached out toward him and then left the movement unfinished. He did not know what to do about Torquil. The harper had betrayed them. But Cradoc wondered, if he had had the power of such perfection in his hands, could he have borne to give it up for anything in the world?

Minutes dragged by and became hours. Their green refuge faded into gray.

"We can go soon," Ferelith said.

"Supper first," Cradoc told her. "Or breakfast."

He reached out and picked a bunch of grapes and offered some to her. With a flicker of surprise, she accepted.

"It's the best we can do," Cradoc said.

He got Torquil to sit up and gave him some of the grapes. The harper had stopped crying, but his eyes were dark and haunted. He said nothing. He could scarcely force himself to eat. When Cradoc remembered the injury to his foot—which seemed to have happened several centuries ago—and asked him if he were fit to go on, he merely nodded. Even then he did not speak.

They moved off downhill, crouching or crawling on hands and knees to keep below the topmost leaves of the vines. It was a tiring way of traveling and they had to stop for frequent rests. Since the horses had passed they had heard nothing of Baric's men. At last, after several hours, they rested, stiff and exhausted, within sound of the river.

"We're on the right of the road," Ferelith murmured. "So the bridge is upstream. You know what I would do," she added, "if I were Baric's men?"

"No, what?"

"Put a guard on the bridge."

She was right, Cradoc realized. Since there were not enough of them for a systematic search, they would try another way.

"Do you want me to go and look?" Ferelith asked.

"I'll go."

"No you won't. They know what you look like. They haven't had a good look at me."

Without waiting for his answer, she slid off between the vines.

"Be careful," he said to her departing back.

Then she was gone. Waiting for her to return, Cradoc felt he should talk to Torquil, but he could not think of anything to say.

Ferelith returned in about half an hour.

"Two of them," she reported, sinking down beside Cradoc. "The two from the farm. I don't know where their leader is. Looking after a bad headache, I hope."

"What do you think we should do?"

Ferelith shook her head.

"We have to get across that river," Cradoc said, almost to himself. "What about you two? Could you swim across?"

Ferelith shrugged.

"Maybe."

Torquil raised frightened eyes to him.

"I can't swim."

"Besides," Ferelith added, "it's no use unless we can think of a way to keep the book dry."

Cradoc sighed deeply.

"We'd better get down there," he decided. "Let's all have a look at it and see what the chances are."

The vines stretched almost to the water's edge. From the cover of the last row they could look out across the wide, smooth expanse of the river, gleaming faintly in the moonlight. Upstream, a bend in the river hid them from the bridge. Downstream, something broke the glassy surface. There was a dark turbulence of which they could not see the cause. There was, of course, nothing so convenient as a boat.

"Let's try downstream," Cradoc said. "There's something there."

As they drew closer they could see that the smooth flow of water was interrupted by rocks, mostly flat and irregularly spaced, but stretched out from one back to the other. Someone reasonably agile could use them to cross.

"There!" Ferelith exclaimed.

"Better than nothing," was Cradoc's opinion.

Torquil shrank back into the cover of the vines.

"I can't!" he gasped. "I'll fall—I told you, I can't swim. You'll have to go on, and leave me here."

"Torquil—" Cradoc was beginning.

"So they can find you and you can tell them everything else they want to know?" Ferelith interrupted. "I wish we could leave you, but we can't, so that's that!"

Torquil gave her one despairing look and covered his face with his hands, sobbing helplessly. Cradoc put a hand on his shoulder.

"Stop it, Ferelith," he said. "That doesn't help. And that doesn't, either, Torquil. You'll have to try, but we'll help you. You'll be all right."

Torquil shook his head.

"It's starting to get light," Cradoc said, ignoring that. "We'll wait until we can see a bit better, but not too long. We'll have to be across and into cover again before daylight."

It seemed a long time that they spent waiting on the edge of the vines, watching the dark expanse of water and the dark sky above. At last the stars paled. More details grew visible around them and they could see the opposite bank more clearly. More vines covered a gentle slope, and a little way upstream they could see a large group of buildings within a wall.

"I wonder what that is," Cradoc said.

No one replied. He got to his feet cautiously and looked around. There was no sign of their enemies.

"Now," he said.

Ferelith rose and joined him.

"I'll go first," she offered. "It doesn't look too difficult. I've got the book, and I suppose I'd better take that wretched harp. Someone will have to."

She tied up her skirts and took the harp. Torquil made no protest. He watched with Cradoc as she ventured out on to the first rock, leaped lightly to a second, and then to a third. Here she turned and looked back.

"Come on!" she called. "There's nothing to it!"

Then she went on, moving neat-footed and never hesitating for more than a few seconds. Shortly she was on the opposite bank. Cradoc turned to Torquil. The harper had recovered a precarious control. At least, he seemed to have accepted the inevitable. Cradoc sent him out first and followed as closely as he could. He was slow and much clumsier than Ferelith, hesitating before he could nerve himself to make each leap from rock to rock. The daylight grew. Cradoc began to have forebodings of what would happen if Baric's men caught them in the middle of the river like this. On the other bank he could see Ferelith looking impatient. He wanted to tell Torquil to hurry, but he bit the words back, not wanting to break his concentration or his courage.

He joined him on a rock that was larger than most and patted his shoulder.

"You're doing well. Look, over halfway."

Torquil glanced back, and then looked at Cradoc, searching his face and seeming about to speak. Then he turned away and tried to move on as if he had suddenly realized Cradoc's urgency. In his haste he misjudged the distance, slipped as he landed on the very edge of the next rock, and fell with a frightened cry. He clawed at the stone as the water surged around him, but before Cradoc could reach him, he was swept away downstream.

17

Cradoc wrenched off his boots and plunged into the river. At first he had lost sight of the harper, until he saw his head break surface a few yards downstream. Cradoc struck out toward him. Torquil was quite helpless in the water, struggling ineffectually to stay afloat. He reached out despairingly toward Cradoc as he drew closer. Cradoc dived to evade the clutching hands, and managed to come up behind Torquil as he was sinking again and grab his shoulders.

"Don't struggle," he gasped in his ear. "I've got you. Just let me do it."

To his relief, the terrified harper seemed able to understand him and obey. Cradoc kicked out across the current. Then he heard a shout. He turned his head to see Ferelith keeping pace with them on the far bank. She was pointing to something downstream. Looking in that direction, Cradoc saw the smooth surface disturbed by rocks again. Beyond that was a kind of dazzling line on the surface of the water and beyond that, nothing except the brightening sky of early morning. The roar of the falls was in his ears. With a sudden chill he realized how strong the current had grown.

"Lord Phoenix, help me now," he murmured.

He tried to judge his distance from the bank and the speed of the river. He knew that he was not making enough headway. Perhaps they could reach a rock and rest for a while. Then he became aware of another head in the water beside him. A strong voice said, "Can you manage, if I take him?"

"Yes."

He was not even sure if that were true.

"Go on, then. I've got him."

Relieved of Torquil's weight, Cradoc found that he could make better progress. The bank drew closer. His feet touched bottom and Ferelith was there, kneeling on the bank, holding out a hand to him. He grasped it and scrambled out.

"Idiot," she said.

Cradoc would have liked to lie still and let everything slip past him like the river. But he forced himself to sit up and see what had happened to Torquil. Not far downstream, the harper was lying face down on the bank with his rescuer stooping over him.

"He'll be all right," he said as Cradoc approached. "Nothing to worry about. Well done."

He was a young man, tall and broad shouldered, with fair hair darkened and flattened by the water. Brilliant blue eyes looked up at Cradoc out of a tanned face.

"Thank you," Cradoc said.

The young man smiled at him.

"I was in the right place, that's all."

He bent over Torquil again. The harper was gasping for air. His struggles to breathe were interspersed with shuddering sobs. The young man reached out to touch his shoulder and his hand seemed to linger on the wet silk of his tunic. He frowned a little, as if he were wondering why he was so unsuitably dressed. But when he looked up, he was smiling again.

"Now you don't want to stand around soaking wet, either of you. You'd better come with me to the Priory."

"Where?"

He gestured upstream to where they could still see the cluster of buildings they had noticed earlier, showing white now in the morning sun.

"The Priory. I come from there. You can have dry clothes and a meal. Then perhaps you can tell us who you are and what all this is about."

"No." Cradoc felt suddenly bone weary at the thought of trying to explain everything. "We can't. We have to hide."

The young man looked puzzled. Ferelith broke in incisively.

"Baric's men are looking for us. There are two waiting for us at the bridge. If we go to your Priory they're bound to find us, and we needn't have bothered with all this nonsense of crossing the river."

The young man looked even more surprised.

"But why—" he began, and stopped himself. "No, later. We'll find a place for you first. Follow me."

He slipped an arm around Torquil and raised him to his feet. Torquil clung to him blindly. Half supporting him, the young man led the way to the very edge of the falls. Cut into the rock—whether deliberately or accidentally Cradoc could not tell—was a narrow stair, which the young man prepared to descend. Torquil shrank back with a whimper of terror.

"It's all right," his rescuer said. "I won't let you fall."

They began to edge their way down, slowly because Torquil was on the verge of panic. Cradoc and Ferelith followed.

"Baric could have had his whole army out here by now," Ferelith muttered.

At the bottom of the stair was a path winding back into the rock behind the falls. Suddenly it widened out into a small cave with three walls of rock and a fourth of falling water. Here the young man let Torquil sink to the ground again.

"I'll be back," he promised, and swiftly returned the way he had come.

"Well!" said Ferelith.

Cradoc sat down heavily and bent his head into his hands. "Ferelith, the book is safe?" he asked.

"No," she retorted caustically, "I threw it in the river. Of course it's safe, idiot, and the harp. Look, Torquil, do you want your harp?"

There was no response from the inert figure of the harper. Ferelith shook her head, half exasperated, half anxious.

"What are we going to do about him?"

"I don't know."

They settled down to wait. Cradoc took off his tunic, wrung the water out of it and spread it out to dry. It was cool in the cave. Torquil had begun to shiver. At last there was the sound of movement along the path and the young man reappeared, laden with provisions. He carried a sealed earthenware pot. He had a leather sack on his back, and under one arm a rolled-up bundle of woollen material which proved to be two long robes of the kind he himself now wore. He gave one to Cradoc who slipped it on thankfully, and took the other over to Torquil.

"Come on, take off that wet tunic and put this on."

At his voice, Torquil half sat up, looking up at him in a daze. He made no move to obey. The young man reached out toward the fastening at the neck of his tunic. At that Torquil started back.

"No! If you knew what I've done, you wouldn't want to help me. You wouldn't want to touch me. You would wish you had left me in the river."

The young man looked at him steadily for a moment, and then shot a thoughtful glance at Cradoc.

"He doesn't—" Cradoc began, but the young man turned away and went on quietly helping Torquil to take off the tunic and put on the robe. After the first protest Torquil submitted as if he were too exhausted to do anything else.

"You'll find soup in that pot," the young man said conversationally. "And bowls in the sack. Perhaps you could get that ready?"

Ferelith obeyed him without a word.

"And after that we can start getting to know each other. My name is Martin; I come from the Priory, as I told you. There isn't anything very interesting to say about me. But I've an idea there's a lot to be said about you. There. That soup is just what we need."

With the lid off the pot, the fragrance was filling the cave. Cradoc thought he had never smelled anything so delicious. Ferelith took a bowl over to Martin who held it for Torquil to drink. The harper was still shivering convulsively.

"Baric's men," Martin said, with more than half his attention still on Torquil. "A troop arrived from Andarre early this morning. They're looking for three fugitives—they described two of you quite well, but they didn't seem too sure about the third.

A serving girl from one of the hill farms, they said."

Ferelith sniffed.

"For some reason they seemed to think you were making for the Priory," Martin continued, "and they didn't believe Father Prior when he told them we had not seen you. They're searching now." He paused. "Don't worry, I made sure I wasn't followed."

"Does anyone else know we're here?" Cradoc asked.

"Of course, I had to tell Father Prior. But he will say nothing, at least for the time. He has no reason to love Baric's men and he wants to know what is behind all this before he makes a decision. So now—" he looked gravely across at Cradoc and Ferelith— "you had better tell me your story."

When Cradoc had finished the story, with interruptions and additions from Ferelith, Martin was silent for a while.

"We have had word of this," he said slowly. "Of a book from Barren which the archpriest of Lindor declared heretical."

"It is not heretical."

Martin nodded. Of all the people who knew about the book, he was the only one not to ask to see it for himself.

"Then if it is truly the Word of God . . . Yes, I can see how this might come about. I suppose you were taking it to Andarre to the Mouse?"

Cradoc looked startled. That was the one thing he had not told.

"Oh, don't worry," Martin said, smiling. "I know all about the Mouse."

"So what are you going to do?" Cradoc asked. "Will you let us go on?"

"That decision rests with Father Prior," Martin replied. "But as I see it, it isn't a question of letting you. You must go on, for none of you will be safe until the book is safely with the Mouse."

He looked down at Torquil, who was crouching at his side. His head and shoulders were bowed with exhaustion and defeat.

"You must help him," he said. "He has suffered a great deal."

"He betrayed us," Ferelith began, but her voice faltered under Martin's stern gaze.

"You have told me you were not his friends. And the book he does not believe in. What reason have you given him to keep faith? Cradoc, if you are to succeed you must forgive him. Will you?"

"Yes, of course."

He spoke Torquil's name and stretched out a hand. Torquil looked up. For a second there was something between them that might have bridged the gulf that had divided them. Then Torquil turned away with a low cry and covered his face with his hands.

"Torquil," Martin said, "despair is a terrible sin. It denies all the beauty of God's creation. It denies all that your life could be in the future. Torquil, if they will forgive you, you must forgive yourself."

The harper shuddered, but made no other response. Martin rested a hand briefly on his shoulder and got to his feet. Cradoc was shocked to see the grief in his face. When he spoke it was with an effort, and his words were strictly practical.

"I shall go now and speak to Father Prior. I think he will wish you to continue. I shall come back after dark—I don't want to risk leading Baric's men here. Get what rest you can and finish the food. I'll bring more when I come back. And Cradoc—" he hesitated, looking down at Torquil—"take care of him. He has great need of healing."

With that, he was gone. Cradoc and Ferelith looked at each other, and then Cradoc moved over to sit beside Torquil. The harper lay face down, silently weeping. He would not reply to anything Cradoc said.

"Let him sleep," Ferelith suggested. "And we should too. We've got to be fit to move on tonight."

Reluctantly Cradoc abandoned his attempts. What Ferelith said was good sense. But he was deeply disturbed, and found that, tired though he was, he could only sleep in snatches. He kept waking to the cave, silent except for the roar of the falls. He saw sunlight dazzling through the water. Ferelith was soundly asleep, and Torquil was lying still, though not, perhaps, asleep. He was shaken from time to time by fits of shivering. He seemed somehow remote—too far away for Cradoc to reach him. Cradoc slept again and dreamed of Torquil being borne away in a dark flood, his hands stretched out for help, but this time there was no one who could help him.

He roused from this last sleep to see Ferelith awake, sitting with her back against the cave wall, reading the book. She smiled at him.

"Have some food," she invited, gesturing toward Martin's sack. "You must be ravenous. I've had mine, but keep some for Torquil."

There was bread and cheese still remaining from the provisions. Cradoc divided it and looked over at Torquil. This time the harper was really asleep. Cradoc took his own portion and went to sit by Ferelith.

"Read to me, then."

Ferelith turned a page and began.

"You that live in the shelter of the Most High and lodge under the shadow of the Almighty, who say, 'The Lord is my safe retreat, my God the fastness in which I trust,' He himself will snatch you away from fowler's snare or raging tempest. He will cover you with his pinions, and you shall find safety beneath his wings."

Cradoc saw that the silver light in the cave had turned to gold. He looked up sharply. Where the curtain of water fell unendingly, he thought he could see, shifting and refracted, the shape of great wings outstretched. Golden rays played across his vision, and one blinding flash shot across the cave. It might have been sunlight reflecting on water, or a gleam from faceted eyes. He cried out, and in an instant it was gone. The gold was no more than the rays of the setting sun striking the waterfall.

"What's the matter?" Ferelith asked.

"I thought—no, it's nothing."

He settled back again. Ferelith read on, but he no longer listened. He was not sure that what he had seen was any more than a trick of the light. Yet in another sense he knew the Lord Phoenix was with them.

And with Torquil, too, he thought. Cradoc wondered if he could ever get the harper to acknowledge that.

He pondered the problem as the golden light faded, leaving the curtain of water an iridescent gray. But no obvious answer suggested itself.

He sprang to his feet as he heard a footstep on the path

outside, but it was only Martin, returning laden as before.

"I came as soon as I could," he said, smiling. "Baric's men are settled at the Priory—not our most welcome visitors! There are two guarding the gate and another two on the bridge, but they needn't bother us. I've brought everything we need for the journey to Andarre."

"We?" Cradoc asked, a sudden hope springing up in his heart.

"Yes," Martin replied, with an even broader smile. "Father Prior has given me leave to go with you. I know a few of the paths to Andarre that even Baric's men don't know. And when we get there, I know how to find the Mouse. Now," he added, "have you eaten? Are you ready to go?"

He crossed the cave swiftly and knelt beside Torquil, rousing him from sleep. The harper half sat up, bewildered and frightened, but he grew quiet at once at Martin's reassurance. While he ate, Martin distributed some of what he had brought— a cloak for Ferelith and strong leather sandals for all three of them. He cleared up all evidence that they had been in the cave and tossed Torquil's discarded tunic down into the falls.

"If they find that," he said, "it might give them a few wrong ideas."

Soon they were ready to leave. They climbed the stair beside the falls and struck into a narrow path through the vineyard.

"The road you meant to take won't be safe any longer," Martin told them. "But I can take you by a different way. Even that might not be completely safe, but it's shorter and it should save us some time."

They began moving in a wide half-circle to avoid the Priory.

"I thought Baric didn't permit the church on his lands?" Cradoc asked.

"But we're not on his lands," Martin explained. "Baric's grandfather and Herrian's great-grandfather established the Priory at the end of the Black Years and gave it lands of its own, equally on both sides of the river. Baric might like to get rid of us, but he daren't do so without provoking war. And none of the Centre lords will do that—not even Baric. They have too much to lose. Besides," he added, with a grin, "at the Priory we make excellent wine and we trade it in Andarre. Even Baric finds the church has its uses."

"Why does he hate it so much?" Ferelith asked.

"Who can tell what is in his heart? But I suspect it's because the church has a power over men's hearts and minds that Baric cannot accept. He doesn't want to share his power with anyone, even the living God. And he will not humble himself to serve, even when God would be his master."

"Like the archpriest in Lindor," Cradoc said suddenly.

Martin looked at him.

"Yes. Cradoc. Perhaps you speak truer than you know. For I believe the archpriest has come to value his own power more than his duty. And when his master called to him in the book you carry, he could not find it in his heart to obey. But we should pity him, for when your book comes to be printed and widely known, he must accept it or lose everything he has."

He halted suddenly and looked around him. The Priory walls were not far away.

"And that will be never if we go on gossiping like farmers on the way to market. Baric's men aren't deaf. We must be quieter from now on."

But everything was silent as they passed the Priory. No challenge rang out from the dark walls. Martin led them through the vineyard, across a strip of meadow, and into the shadow of trees. In a few minutes the Priory was out of sight and they faced the secret places of the forest.

19

All that night they saw and heard no one. Even under the darkness of the trees, Martin trod confidently and the others followed him. Once a disturbance in the undergrowth brought them to a halt, but it was only a badger lumbering across their path.

For most of the night the forest track had wound upward. As morning crept through the trees they saw they were in a wild land of rocks and falling water with twisted shrubs rooted in crevices. Taller trees crowded where the soil was richer. Cradoc found it indescribably beautiful, and lonelier than he could imagine, as if they were the first people ever to set foot there.

"Not many travelers use this road," Martin said, answering his thought. "That path you would have taken follows the valley, but we can save time by crossing the ridge and we'll avoid Baric's men."

As the sky grew brighter they began looking for somewhere to rest. For some time Torquil had been clinging to Martin's arm, and now he stumbled along in a haze of fatigue. Martin was almost carrying him by the time they stopped. From the top of an overhanging rock, trailing plants hung down and formed a screen with room for them to lie concealed behind it. A stream flowed near its foot and they splashed across it to reach the shelter of the rock. Martin let Torquil sink to the ground and looked around approvingly.

"We're well hidden here. I don't think we need to keep watch. All the same . . . you others sleep. I don't feel like it, not right away."

Cradoc and Ferelith were glad enough to settle down, and Torquil had already slid into unconsciousness. When Cradoc woke, the sun was high. Ferelith still slept. Martin was sitting with his back to the rock and Torquil lay with his head in his lap. Martin's eyes seemed intent on something beyond the screen of grasses. Following his gaze, Cradoc saw that he was watching a pair of red squirrels chasing each other through the nearby trees. After a moment, Martin turned and smiled at him.

"Hungry?"

"Yes!"

"Pass me that bag."

Cradoc did so. They shared bread and fruit as they watched the squirrels. Torquil was sleeping uneasily and sometimes seemed almost to rise up or speak a few disjointed words. Cradoc thought he looked feverish and he still shivered spasmodically.

"Is he ill?" he asked anxiously.

Martin shook his head.

"Not seriously—at least I hope it's no more than exhaustion and the shock of the river yesterday. Of course, he shouldn't be here. If I had him in the Priory, I could care for him." He paused, and added, "No, his real sickness is in the mind."

"But what can we do?"

"You want to help him?"

"Yes, of course I do."

Martin smiled sadly.

"It isn't easy. Not even as easy as risking your life for him in the river. That was a fine thing to do, Cradoc. But it came of your courage, your goodness of heart. And Torquil knows you would have done it for anyone, even your bitterest enemy, because of what you are."

Cradoc scarcely noticed the praise. He was too intent on the problem of Torquil.

"I don't blame him for what he did at the farm," he said. "I might have done the same if I'd been hard pressed. But before that—in the court—he was deliberately unpleasant to us and I don't understand why. Still, we could forget all that and be friends. But he won't let us."

"Perhaps he doesn't know how."

Cradoc was not sure he understood that.

CHAPTER 19

"You have to learn love, Cradoc, as you learn everything else. You had someone to teach you—family, friends—and you can learn it from our Lord. Torquil has never known Him. I think he has never learned to love, or to trust."

"Can we teach him?"

"I don't know. Perhaps in time. He needs us now, and that may make it easier. But it must grow out of love—even pity isn't enough." He sighed faintly. "I wish I could hear him play the harp."

"I heard him once—the night we left the court. It was beautiful."

"A gift of God—and yet it led him into treachery."

"That wasn't his fault."

Martin lifted his head.

"Oh, no. Don't let your pity for him mislead you, Cradoc. We may understand what he did, but it was wrong and he knows it. What he doesn't know is that there is forgiveness—there is always forgiveness."

He sighed again more deeply and passed his hand gently over Torquil's hair.

"Somehow, before we part, I must convince him of that."

They spent one more night on the road. By the following morning they were among farms and fields—a well-tilled, prosperous land. As their path descended they began to pass early farm workers who looked curiously at the little group.

"We can't hide any longer," Martin said. "And we're only a few miles from Andarre. I think we should go on if you can."

That was really addressed to Torquil. Cradoc and Ferelith had found it easy to keep up with his slower pace. The harper, who was once again supported by Martin, raised sunken eyes to his face.

"If we could rest a little first. . . ." he suggested timidly.

"Yes, we can rest, and talk, too. We need to decide what we're going to do next."

They sat in the shelter of a hedge to rest and eat.

"We must come to Andarre by day in any case," Martin told them. "The gates are guarded and closed at night."

"Then we'll be stopped there!" Cradoc exclaimed in dismay. Martin frowned.

"Perhaps. Of course they may not expect you in Andarre. But the guards are bound to keep a lookout just in case."

"Then how can we get in?"

"That will be difficult."

"If only they didn't know about us!" Ferelith broke in. "Everything was so much simpler before. Oh, I'm sorry, Torquil," she added hastily. "I didn't mean . . ."

But they had all seen Torquil flinch as if from a blow. And they knew that Ferelith had spoken the truth.

Martin thought for a while in silence and then straightened up as if he had come to a decision. Cradoc turned to him expectantly.

"I think I can see a way. Ferelith, Baric's men know next to nothing about you. None of them has had a good look at you, so you must take the book into Andarre."

Ferelith nodded and patted her apron pocket where the book was concealed.

"Cradoc, you change back into your own clothes and go with her. Take Torquil's harp, too—is that all right, Torquil?" The harper murmured assent. "Musicians travel. No one will see anything strange in that."

Cradoc grinned.

"I just hope no one asks me for a song!"

"You two can go on ahead and Torquil and I will follow. With Torquil dressed like that, the guards won't look at him twice."

"And where shall we go once we're inside?" Ferelith asked. "Remember, we've never set foot in Andarre."

"I haven't forgotten. There's an inn that we always use when we come to Andarre from the Priory. The innkeeper is a friend of the church, for all Baric's forbidding it. It's about a quarter of a mile up the main street that leads from the gate. Look for the Sign of the Phoenix."

"The Phoenix!" Cradoc exclaimed.

Martin gave him a look of amusement at his surprise.

"God doesn't deal in coincidences," was all he said.

20

Cradoc and Ferelith reached Andarre before midday. Not long after they left Martin and Torquil, their track joined a wider road and the city came into sight. Cradoc remembered Lindor as shining white in sunlight with flowers spilling over garden walls. In contrast, Andarre was gray and brooding. It was larger, too, and seemed stronger, as if it reflected the power of its lord.

Before they reached the city, the air was filled with the muted roaring Cradoc remembered from Barren. From somewhere beyond the city, a silver ship lifted into the sky. As he had done so many times on his own world, Cradoc watched it out of sight. But he could hardly recall what it had felt like to long to travel on one of them. So many more important things had happened since then.

At the city gates there were many travelers passing to and fro, but Cradoc's hope that they might slip through the gates unnoticed was disappointed. Everyone who entered Andarre had to stop and be identified.

"Musicians, are you?" said a bored guard. "Well, if you go to the court, mind you don't play any wrong notes. My lord Baric can be very touchy."

"He certainly won't have heard music like ours," Ferelith retorted pertly.

To Cradoc's relief the guard waved them through, but as they made their way through the press of people around the gates, he noticed one man observing them with intense interest. He was slight and dark, with a thin, intelligent face. He wore a gray cloak and hood. Cradoc clutched Ferelith's arm to point him out, but when he turned back to look for him the man had disappeared in the crowd.

"Someone was watching us."

"Well, that's what we expected. There's no need to tell the whole of Andarre about it. Just keep going."

"There are more guards around, too," Cradoc muttered, though he obeyed Ferelith and resisted the temptation to stare around him.

Ferelith was looking for the Sign of the Phoenix and made no reply. Then Cradoc heard the sound he had been dreading—a shout from behind them. He turned to see a unit of Baric's guards. One of them gestured in his direction, and they began thrusting their way through the crowds. Ferelith grabbed Cradoc's wrist.

"Run!"

It was hard to move fast on the main street. But Ferelith, who had kept her wits about her, dragged Cradoc to a corner and down an alley away from the crowd. At first they thought they had escaped, but then the guards appeared at the entrance to the alley. Cradoc and Ferelith fled around the next corner. Then they were dodging breathlessly down lanes and narrow passages, all the while hearing the pounding feet of their pursuers.

They were drawing closer.

"Can't . . . keep this up," Ferelith gasped.

"Go on—with the book. I'll try to hold them."

"No. Too many."

They rounded the next corner and stopped dead in dismay. The passage widened into a kind of courtyard. The buildings were crumbling and derelict. There was no obvious way out. Cradoc had only just time to drag Ferelith into the shelter of a pile of stones before the guards appeared. There were four of them. Two of them remained by the entrance while the others began to search.

"They'll find us," Ferelith whispered.

"I know. Hide the book. If we haven't got it on us, perhaps—"

Cradoc was interrupted by a low whistle. He could not see where it had come from. It was repeated. It seemed to come out of the ground. Then he saw. In the wall nearby there was a low archway closed by wooden shutters. But one of the shutters was open a crack, and Cradoc could just make out a face in the shadows inside.

"Over here," a low voice said.

The shutter gaped wider. With a glance over his shoulder at the guards who were searching over the other side of the courtyard, Cradoc pushed Ferelith across to the opening and slid down after her into the darkness inside.

An unseen hand closed the shutter. At first Cradoc could see nothing. But after a moment he could hear the footsteps of the guards and their voices.

"No sign of them."

"They came in here."

"Then they must have gone over that wall."

"If Baric finds out we found them and lost them again . . ."

Both voices and footsteps receded.

By this time Cradoc's eyes were adjusting to the dim light. He was in a cellar—a bare room with dirty walls that had once been whitewashed. Standing in front of him was a young man. Looking at him, Cradoc wondered if Baric's guards might have been preferable. He was dark, good-looking in a predatory way, dressed in a tunic that had once been richly embroidered velvet. Now it was ragged and stiff with dirt. In his fingers he was absent-mindedly twirling a long, vicious-looking knife.

"Good afternoon," he said, smiling.

"It was good of you to help us," Cradoc began, awkwardly. "Do you—"

"So Baric's guards had an interest in you," the young man interrupted. "I wonder why?"

"I haven't the faintest idea," Ferelith interrupted snappishly. Cradoc guessed she was afraid too. "But we didn't feel like staying to find out, did we? And we're very grateful to you, but really we have to go now. So if you could . . ."

"Just a minute." The man's voice was soft and he was still smiling pleasantly, but Cradoc could feel how dangerous he was. "You can't go just like that. Oh, no. You'll have to come and pay your respects to my master."

"Who's he?" Cradoc asked.

"Who—oh, you must be strangers to Andarre. My master is Lord Tybalt—just as important a man as Baric, in his way. More important, you might say. More important to you, just now. Come with me."

He gestured courteously toward the inner door, indicating that Ferelith and Cradoc should go first. Cradoc was uncomfortably aware of the knife point at his back. Their guide shepherded them along a passage and through another door into a much larger room lit by lamps. At a table in the center, spread with the remains of a meal, a man was sitting—an enormously fat man with a straggle of red hair around an otherwise bald head. As they entered he looked up, and a benign smile crept across his face. Cradoc was not reassured, for he had seen the small, cruel eyes.

"What's all this?" he asked.

"Visitors, master." The first man's tone had grown crisp and efficient. "Baric's men were after them. I helped them escape."

"That was very kind of you."

He wiped his hands on his greasy leather vest, pushed away his plate, and eased himself back in his chair. For a moment he looked over his two prisoners and then seemed to lose interest and began banging his wine cup on the table. A terrified-looking girl came out of the shadows and refilled it from a jug.

"We thank you for your help. . . ." Ferelith began.

A short, chopping gesture reduced her to silence. The fat man resumed his scrutiny and then asked, "Do you know who I am?"

"You're . . . Lord Tybalt?" Cradoc managed to say.

"That's my name. But do you know who I am?"

"No."

The young man's knife glittered in front of his face.

"Around here we call him 'Master.' "

"No, Master."

Tybalt shifted his bulk in the chair.

"Then I'll tell you. I'm . . . in charge of things around here. Baric may be lord of Andarre, but he can't be everywhere at once, so I shoulder some of the responsibility for him. You might say that I'm his viceroy."

He smiled broadly as if he liked that word. "Yes, his viceroy."

"You mean you're going to hand us over to him?" Ferelith asked.

Cradoc put his hand over hers warningly.

"Yes, your pretty friend does talk too much," Tybalt said. "Well, my dear, I might do just that if I thought it would do me most good. But I don't know. Have you searched them?" he asked his lieutenant.

"No, Master."

"Then do it now. And relieve the lad of that harp to start with. It must be very heavy to carry."

The young man obeyed and handed the harp to the girl who scurried off into the shadows with it. In the midst of their other trouble, the thought flashed through Cradoc's mind that he was never going to be able to face Torquil. The man searched him and took the silver pin that fastened his tunic. But to his relief, after a brief examination, left him the wooden cross. He then moved on to Ferelith and took from her the purse which Lord Herrian had given to her. Finally, from her apron pocket, he took the book.

Tybalt beckoned, and the young man crossed the room and put it in his hands. He flicked over the pages. Something about the way he did it told Cradoc he could not read.

"Please let us keep it," he began, hoping he could bluff his way out. "It's not important—not valuable."

Tybalt looked up at him, the small eyes suddenly shrewd.

"But it's important to you, lad, isn't it? And it might be valuable to someone else—to Baric, say? And if so, it might be valuable to me."

He put the book on the table and sat looking at it. Cradoc did not dare to speak.

"Baric's been looking for a book," Tybalt went on. "An old book that came from Barren, so they say. An evil book, so the archpriest of Lindor said. Oh, I hear all the gossip. Now, it wouldn't be right to let an evil book just go wandering around loose, would it? I couldn't sleep at nights with that on my conscience."

"It's not evil!" Cradoc could not prevent the words bursting out. "It's the Word of God."

"The Word of God? But Baric doesn't like that, either. He's freed us from all these old superstitions. And as his viceroy, I don't think I can let you keep it. No, my duty tells me to take it to Baric."

"So that he'll pay you for it!" Ferelith exclaimed.

"Lad, you want to tell your friend to mind her tongue. Or I might have to keep her quiet some other way. As for paying me, I might see my way to accepting a small token of his gratitude."

"We could pay you!" Cradoc interrupted desperately.

Tybalt grinned derisively.

"Oh, yes?"

"Not now. But if you send us to the Phoenix Inn, you could—"

Tybalt was shaking his head.

"No, lad. I told you, it's my duty. I have to do my duty. The book goes to Baric."

He slid even further back in his chair, closed his eyes, and flapped a hand wearily in their direction.

"Go on, get rid of them. They're annoying me."

"But listen—" Cradoc cried.

He broke off as Tybalt's lieutenant twisted his arm behind him and showed the knife. For a second he thought Ferelith was going to spring at him.

"No, don't!" he gasped. "It's no use."

Cradoc felt the prick of the knife at his throat.

"Sensible." He jerked his head at Ferelith. "Go on. Out."

They were bundled back into the passage and up a flight of stairs. At the head of it was a door which opened on to a narrow street. The young man thrust them outside. Cradoc fell to his knees on the stones. The door slammed shut behind them.

21

Cradoc got to his feet and began dusting himself down. Ferelith was pounding furiously on the closed door.

"Stop it," Cradoc said wearily. "It's no use."

"Then what are we going to do?"

"There's nothing we can do except find the Phoenix and tell Martin."

Reluctantly Ferelith turned away from the door and then turned back.

"Cradoc, the book's in there! We can't leave it."

"We have to. Even if we got back inside we couldn't do anything. They would kill us. You know they would. Then Martin would never know what had happened to the book."

He was afraid Ferelith would think he was a coward, but after a brief hesitation she nodded despairingly.

"You're right. Come on."

"Just a minute."

He crossed the street from the building they had left and looked around carefully. He was trying to find a landmark that would fix the place so that he could find it again in case Martin thought there was anything he could do. There was nothing particularly unusual, and after a moment he gave up and followed Ferelith along the street.

They had no idea where their flight from Baric's men had taken them, and it was late afternoon before they found the Phoenix. They did their best to avoid being seen by guards and did not dare to ask anyone the way. At last they reached the inn. Cradoc stood for a moment looking up at the creaking, weatherworn sign where he could still pick out a hint of gold.

He felt confused and very tired.

"What are you waiting for?" Ferelith asked.

"I don't know."

He led the way inside and stood looking around the crowded room. There was no sign of Martin. He thought he caught a glimpse of the stranger in the gray cloak who had shown such interest in them at the city gates, but he could not be sure. Then he forgot about it as Ferelith tugged at his arm.

"I've spoken to the innkeeper. Martin's upstairs."

Martin was in one of the inn's bedrooms, sitting by Torquil who lay sleeping. He sprang to his feet as Cradoc and Ferelith came in.

"At last! I thought something—" He broke off. Ferelith burst into tears. "Something has happened. Come and tell me."

He closed the door and put an arm around Ferelith as he led her to a seat. Torquil, disturbed by the noise and movement, stirred and sat up.

"Well?" Martin asked.

It was left to Cradoc to tell the story. Martin listened attentively, not interrupting.

"So we've lost the book," Cradoc finished hopelessly. "This . . . Tybalt is going to sell it to Baric and that will be the end of it."

Martin was frowning slightly. At first he said nothing.

"Why did God let it happen?" Cradoc asked, sudden bitterness threatening to overwhelm him. "He showed me where to find the book on Barren and brought us here through all our dangers and now this. It doesn't make sense."

Martin looked at him with a tired smile.

"I'm afraid God doesn't work like that. He won't do it all for us. We still have to face danger or weariness or sheer misfortune. You could have lost the book a dozen times before now. And remember this—" A little energy crept back into his voice. "If Baric's guard had caught you, Baric would have the book now. As it is, there's still a chance."

All at once Cradoc felt immeasurably encouraged.

"What are you going to do?" he asked.

"Not a miracle, you can be sure of that. But I know Tybalt, or at least I know of him. And I know one or two things about him that may be useful. I'm going to see if I can have a word with him."

"I'll come with you."

Martin shook his head.

"Baric's men are still looking for you. And I think I can handle Tybalt better alone. You two stay here and rest. You can have a meal if you want, but you'd better eat it up here. And don't worry. We aren't finished yet."

Cradoc had to agree. And even Ferelith, who had stopped crying, made no protest. Martin was about to go with a word of farewell, when Torquil reached out a hand to stop him.

"Martin . . ." He was speaking with difficulty. "Martin, you're in danger, too."

Martin smiled at him.

"Nonsense."

"It's not. You've been seen with me. . . ."

"That doesn't mean anything. If I'm questioned, I met you on the road. I gave you a helping hand. But I don't know who you are or what your business was." Gently he took Torquil's hands. "It's all right. There's nothing to be afraid of."

Then he was gone. Ferelith closed the door behind him.

Torquil sat looking after him as if he would have liked to follow. Cradoc touched his arm.

"Torquil, I'm sorry about the harp."

Torquil averted his face. He was obviously very upset. But after a moment he whispered, "It doesn't matter."

Cradoc sat beside him.

"Go back to sleep. Martin might be back by the time you wake."

The eyes that rested briefly on Cradoc's face were absolutely without hope. Cradoc sighed. Life on the farm on Barren had been hard, but it had been simple. He had disliked the farmer and Jerd the overseer. He got along with his fellow workers and revered Father Huon. He had never experienced anything so complex as his feelings about Torquil. His first hostility had been tempered by wonder at Torquil's music and by pity once their journey began. He still could not have said whether he liked Torquil, but he knew there had been growing since Torquil's betrayal a painful and difficult love. And he had no idea how to express it or what to do with it.

Feeling that he must make some effort to reach him, however clumsy, Cradoc began to speak again.

"Torquil, we're here, in Andarre. You needn't torment yourself anymore."

Torquil turned to look at him.

"That doesn't make any difference. Besides, it isn't over. You lost the book because Baric's men recognized you. That's because of me. Ferelith was right."

He spoke with bitter desolation. But Cradoc could not help being a little encouraged. At least talking about it was better than silence and fits of tortured weeping.

"You don't have to worry—" he began.

"I betrayed you," Torquil interrupted. "Nothing can ever wipe that out. Cradoc, I've never thanked you for saving my life. I do thank you, but it would have been better if you had left me in the river."

"No—" Cradoc protested.

"What use is my life now?"

"You'll go back to Herrian. He said he would receive you."

Torquil turned away restlessly. Behind him Cradoc could hear faint sounds of Ferelith moving around the room. Torquil went on, speaking in no more than a whisper.

"I don't know . . . when he knows what I've done, he may not want me. Besides, I don't want to go back. Cradoc, you know what I was there. There's no one who would be glad to see me."

"Lord Herrian—"

"Lord Herrian only wanted me for my music. No one has ever wanted me for anything else."

"There's Martin," Cradoc suggested.

Torquil turned his head away, but not before Cradoc had seen the tears spill over.

"Martin will go back to the Priory and I'll never see him again.

Compassionately Cradoc reached out and took his hand. But Torquil withdrew it.

"I'm all right." With a visible effort he forced back the tears and looked up at Cradoc once again. "I'll go back to Lord Herrian if I can. What else is there?"

"And you still have your music."

"Yes—but I'll never play again without remembering I sold you to save it."

Cradoc shot an agonized glance at Ferelith. She was sitting by the window, her chin in her hands. She was watching them, but not offering him any help.

Desperately Cradoc said, "There is a way out. Our Lord died so there should be a way out. To set us free in some way from all the wrong we do. . . ." He stumbled, knowing he was expressing this badly. "Martin could explain it better," he finished. "And it would tell you in the book."

Torquil's tormented eyes were fixed on him. "But it isn't true."

"Martin believes it."

His glance wavered then and his voice was unsteady as he asked, "But what difference would it make?"

"It means a fresh start. It means you could forget all about what happened at the farm or at Herrian's court. You needn't go on carrying that awful burden anymore. . . ."

He broke off, appalled, as Torquil turned from him convulsively. His hands were over his face and tearing sobs came from him, causing his whole body to shake. Cradoc could say nothing, only reach out and put a hand on his shoulder. But there was no sign that Torquil felt comforted by it. Cradoc sat still and silent until the fit had subsided.

Although he tried to reach out again to offer friendship and reassurance, the harper would not respond. At last Cradoc withdrew and went to sit beside Ferelith.

"I don't know what to do," he said in a low voice.

"I'm not surprised." There was an edge to her tone. "Oh, Cradoc, I know that we should try to forgive him and help him, but it's difficult. He makes it difficult. He's been nothing but a nuisance ever since—"

She broke off.

"What's the matter?" Cradoc asked.

"I thought I heard something."

They listened, and a few seconds later Cradoc too heard a sound—a faint scratching at the door. He thought of Baric and his men and the gray-cloaked man he had seen watching them. But the sound was too uncertain for that. He exchanged a glance with Ferelith and then strode across the room to the door and flung it open.

Cradoc stood still in astonishment. Outside the door, looking up at him with frightened eyes, was the girl he had seen in Tybalt's cellar. Quickly he looked up and down the passage. She was alone. He grasped her arm and pulled her into the room. Ferelith rose, an exclamation on her lips.

"What are you doing here?" Cradoc asked. "What do you want?"

Before the girl could answer, Ferelith added, "How did you find us? Did you follow us?"

The girl pushed back her mass of tangled hair. She was thin and her dress was worn and patched, but it was at least clean.

"No," she said slowly. "No, I didn't follow you. But you spoke to Tybalt of the Phoenix. As soon as I could get away I came here to look for you."

"Why?" Cradoc asked.

She twisted her hands nervously in her apron. Cradoc suddenly realized how hostile he and Ferelith must sound.

"Sit down," he said more quietly. "There's nothing to be afraid of. What's your name?"

"Alys."

"I'm Cradoc, and this is Ferelith. Now sit down and tell us why you're here."

Hesitantly she balanced on the very edge of a chair.

"That book Tybalt took from you," she began. "It's important to you?"

"Yes."

"Do you want it back?"

"How can you—"

Cradoc had started to speak when Ferelith interrupted. "Of course we want it back. Are you telling us you've got it?"

Alys looked around at her, more nervous than ever.

"Oh, no. No, I wouldn't dare. But I know where it is."

"We know where it is, too," Ferelith said acidly. "On its way to Baric in Tybalt's pocket."

"But it isn't."

"Where is it, then?" Cradoc asked tensely.

The tension was shared by everyone in the room. Cradoc noticed that even Torquil had been drawn out of his self-absorption and was listening.

"Tybalt wouldn't take it to Baric," the girl explained. "Not right away. He doesn't trust Baric. He doesn't trust anybody. He would want to make a deal first. I think he's gone there now, but before he left he took the book and the harp away to a safe place—an empty house near the cellar. He's used it before. He left Rual to guard it."

"Is Rual the other man who was there with Tybalt?"

"Yes, the one who brought you in."

"And why are you telling us all this?" Ferelith asked.

The girl's gaze flickered across to her and then to Cradoc and Torquil.

"If you want to get it back," she said at last, her voice scarcely above a whisper, "I could show you where to go."

There was a sudden silence. It was Ferelith who broke it sharply.

"No. It's a trap."

"No!" Alys protested.

"It may not be a trap," Cradoc said to Ferelith. "Even if it is, don't we have to risk it? If there's even the slightest chance of getting the book back. . . ."

"Then suppose she tells us what she came here for. What does she get out of it?"

Cradoc turned to the girl. She looked close to tears. He knew Ferelith was frightening her, and he understood it was because she was so upset about the book.

"Well?" he asked, trying to make his voice gentle.

Alys reached out and clasped his hand.

"I hate Tybalt," she said. "I want to leave him, but he'll never let me go. I'll take you to the book if you'll help me."

"What do you want?"

"A place to go where he'll never find me."

Cradoc smiled at her.

"Yes, of course." He looked up at Ferelith. "You could take her to Lindor to your lady."

He prayed that Ferelith would not reject the suggestion out of hand. To his relief she did not, though she sounded doubtful.

"I could . . . my lady would receive her if she's telling the truth."

"I am." As if the idea of going to Lindor had given her hope, her spirit seemed to revive. "Why else would I be here? To lead you into a trap for Tybalt? What would Tybalt want with you? He's got all he wants from you. That's why he let you go."

"Unless Baric wants us," Cradoc suggested, half to himself. "No," he added. "He wants the book, that's all. If he wanted us, he could come and get us. Ferelith, I think she's right. I'm prepared to trust her, anyway. I think we should go with her."

Ferelith hesitated a moment. Alys, seeing the hesitation, suddenly sprang to her feet.

"I know what the book is, you know," she said, her voice low and shaken with what she was feeling. "I wasn't always with Tybalt. I've been taught some things, and I know that if our Lord came here, to Andarre, it would be to people like us he would come—like me and Tybalt and Rual, not to Baric, not to the court. Perhaps not even to you."

She pressed her hands to her lips as if she was suddenly afraid she had said too much.

"She's right," Cradoc said quietly. "We ought to go with her."

Ferelith nodded.

"All right."

"Shouldn't we wait for Martin?" Torquil suggested shyly.

Ferelith gave him a look as if she had not admitted him to the discussion. "No time," she said abruptly. "If we go, we go now. You can tell him about it."

"But I want to come with you."

He got up, pulled on his robe and began looking for his sandals. "She said my harp is there. I must get it back."

Cradoc and Ferelith exchanged a glance.

"All right," Cradoc said, before Ferelith could object.

"But you do as we tell you," she added.

With Alys leading, they left the room quietly. They crept downstairs, out of the Phoenix, and crossed the courtyard to a back entrance leading into a narrow, deserted street. Looking up and down, Cradoc could see no one. He did not think Baric's men could possibly be following them.

"This way," Alys said.

She set off down the street. Ferelith drew back to walk at Cradoc's side.

"I know I'm being horrible to everybody," she murmured. "I can't help it. I'm so worried. To come this far and then lose it! And if we hadn't—"

"It's all right," Cradoc interrupted. "I understand. I feel just as bad myself. But at least we're doing something about it."

"If we aren't running into even worse trouble."

They followed Alys through a network of back streets. The sun had set and the light was fading. Cradoc soon lost his sense of direction. He was so lightheaded with weariness, he was not sure if the gathering shadows were real or in his own mind. He was sure he would never find his way back to the Phoenix alone. At last, when there was still enough light left to see by, Alys stopped at the entrance to a courtyard.

"The house straight ahead of you," she whispered. "I'll wait here. I daren't go any further. If they see me . . ."

"Yes, you stay out of sight," Cradoc agreed. "We can deal with Rual if we have to."

Nevertheless, he did not feel at all confident as he led the way across the courtyard. He was thankful for the gathering darkness that hid their approach, though he was in the state of mind that expects an enemy in every shadow. The house they were headed for was apparently not in use. The door was sagging off its hinges and the window shutters had boards nailed across them. Cradoc was beginning to wonder if Alys had told the truth when he noticed light shining through the chinks of one boarded window.

With an intake of breath he touched Ferelith's arm and pointed it out. She slid forward. On tiptoe she managed to put her eye to a crack. Then she turned away, shaking her head in disappointment.

"I can't see much."

"Then we'll go in."

He pushed his way past the sagging door. Ferelith and Torquil followed. The passage in which he stood was half-blocked with rubbish. He could just make out cobwebs hanging from the ceiling. They brushed against his face as he moved forward. He heard a stifled sound of disgust from Ferelith. At the end of the passage was a door outlined by a hairline of light. Cradoc paused, swallowed, and pushed it open.

Only a single oil lamp was burning, but it seemed dazzlingly bright after the gloom outside. By its light he could see Torquil's harp set on an old, broken-backed chair near the door. There was a table, and sitting on a chair half-turned to the door was Rual. There was no sign of the book.

23

At Cradoc's entrance, Rual got to his feet, and a smile slowly spread across his face. His knife had appeared from nowhere. He weighed it reflectively in his hand as he looked Cradoc and the others over.

"Well," he said at last, when no one else spoke. "This is interesting. I didn't expect you. I didn't think you would have the wits to find this place . . . or did someone tell you?" An ugly look crossed his face. "That whining little Alys—"

"Never mind that," Cradoc interrupted.

He took a pace forward to let Ferelith and Torquil into the room. Lamplight flickered along the knife blade as Rual held it poised to strike.

"No nearer," he said. "Talk from there if you want to talk."

"There's nothing to talk about."

Cradoc was trying to sound confident. But in reality he was suddenly afraid they had taken on more than they could manage. And where was the book?

"We've come for what Tybalt took from us."

Rual smiled and gestured toward the harp.

"Take it—if you can."

"And the book?"

"The book? Is that here?"

Uneasily Cradoc realized that perhaps the book was not there. He was sure now that Alys had not lied, but she might have been mistaken. There was nowhere in sight for the book to be hidden except for a pile of old sacks and rubbish near the unused fireplace. Unless, perhaps Rual was carrying it himself. Cradoc examined him carefully trying to guess. The once-fine tunic was bulky enough to conceal it. Cradoc could not be sure.

"We know you have it," he began.

"Then I've told you—come and take it. There are three of you. What are you waiting for? Though there doesn't seem to be much fight in any of you. Why don't you—"

He broke off as Cradoc sprang at him. The knife flashed; Cradoc felt a sensation like a red-hot needle being drawn down his forearm. He grabbed the hand that held the knife and bore down on it. Dimly he realized that Ferelith and Torquil had joined the struggle.

"Hold him," he gasped. "Search—the book—"

Rual threw him off and he rolled over on the floor. Scrambling to his knees he saw Rual crouched over the knife, holding off the other two. Cradoc flung himself on him from behind, wrapping his arms around him, trying to keep a grip on him and feel for the book at the same time. It was not there. He was almost sure of that when Rual broke his grasp and thrust him back against he table. It rocked and tipped over. Cradoc missed his footing and went down with it. There was a blinding pain in his head. He fought against a surging darkness, knowing somehow it was important not to give in to it. Somewhere above his head a voice was crying out. Then it faded.

He thought afterward he never lost consciousness entirely or not for long. His next sensation was of being carried and then set down. Cool outdoor air began to revive him. He realized he was lying on the uneven cobbles of the courtyard.

"Cradoc! Cradoc!"

It was Ferelith's voice. "All right," he tried to say. He sat up, but his head began to swim again. He wanted to be sick, but he gritted his teeth and held on to self-control. Soon he was able to look around. Already people were gathering in the courtyard and it was easy to see the reason. From the house they had left, a plume of smoke was rising and there was a red flicker of fire.

"What happened?" he asked.

"You fell and hit your head," Ferelith explained. She was kneeling beside him with an arm around his shoulders. "The table went over and the lamp and the oil spilled. That stupid

Rual ran off. Torquil and I got you out. Torquil—"

She stood up and looked around.

"Cradoc—he's gone!"

With an effort Cradoc got to his feet.

"Where?"

"I don't know, I didn't see. Cradoc, you don't suppose he's gone back in there? His harp is still there, and—oh, Cradoc, the book!"

But Cradoc was already racing back toward the building.

The passage was hazy with smoke, but the flames had not yet reached it. From the door of the room at the end more smoke was pouring out. As Cradoc groped his way through, smoke stung his eyes and caught at his throat.

"Torquil!"

There was no answer to his choking cry. Just inside the door he caught sight of Torquil's harp, as yet untouched by flames. He reached for it, but already he was transfixed by what he saw across the room. Where the table had stood the walls and floor were ablaze. Seemingly in the midst of the flames, near the pile of rubbish that was now flaring up fiercely, was a kneeling figure— Torquil, beating frantically at something he held close to him. For one terrible moment Cradoc thought the fire was devouring him. Then he realized he was holding the book, desperately trying to crush out the flames that licked over the cover and along the fragile, brittle pages. As Cradoc stumbled toward him, he saw the flames die. Torquil raised his head and held out the book to him.

"It's all right—look."

"Idiot!" Cradoc snapped, hauling him to his feet. "Come on."

He could scarcely speak, scarcely even breath as the smoke thickened. His eyes were streaming. His senses were reeling. He was not sure of the way to the door. Torquil, who had been in there longer, was in an even worse state. Clinging to each other they staggered across the room. They found the door, only to be beaten back by a surge of flames as the wall between the room and the passage gave way. They retreated a pace or two, but there was no escape that way. The window was still untouched, but the shutter was firmly nailed in place.

"We'll have to go through," Cradoc gasped. "Cover your face. It can't be more than a few steps."

Though he looked terrified, Torquil nodded.

"I'm ready."

But it was more than they could do. The intense heat forced them back and they could retreat no further. Their refuge at the end of the passage grew smaller every second. Flakes of fire drifted down on them. The flames seemed to reach out hungrily toward them. Torquil had hidden his face and Cradoc tightened his arm around him as he still peered through the smoke and the blaze, reluctant to give up hope until the last. So it was that he saw the moment when the flames parted and spread from wall to wall in the form of immense wings. Between them the majestic head took shape, the fiery plumes streaming far above their heads. Beneath the wings was cool air and darkness. Beyond was the door to the courtyard.

"Torquil," Cradoc whispered.

The harper looked up and Cradoc heard him catch his breath. For a moment neither of them could move. Then Cradoc urged Torquil forward.

They passed unharmed beneath the arch of fire. But under the shelter of the wings Torquil paused and looked up wonderingly into the luminous eyes. And for all the marvel of the Phoenix, it was his face that Cradoc looked at: innocent, joyful, and at peace. Then he remembered where they were. Dragging at Torquil, he brought him out into the open air. Behind them, with a roar of flame, the roof fell in and a column of fiery sparks billowed upward into the night sky.

Cradoc saw none of that. He and Torquil stumbled and fell on the stones of the courtyard. Torquil's robe was aflame. Cradoc crushed out the flames and knelt beside him. Torquil was still clutching the book. Now he held it out to Cradoc.

"It's safe," he whispered. "Give it to Martin."

"Yes, I will." Cradoc took it, almost unaware that he had done so. "But Torquil—"

"I've been such a nuisance," the harper interrupted. He spoke so faintly that Cradoc had to bend down to hear him. His parched lips moved into a smile.

"I'm sorry."

He reached up and touched the wooden cross that hung between them from Cradoc's neck. For the first time Cradoc saw the ruin of his hands. Forcing back the horror he felt, he took off the cross and passed the thong over Torquil's head. The harper laid a hand protectively over it. He gave a faint sigh and his head fell back.

Cradoc bent over him anxiously. At his side Ferelith asked, "Is he—" and could not go on.

Then there was another disturbance. Martin was shouldering his way through the crowd nearby. He dropped to his knees by Torquil's side.

"Torquil!" he exclaimed. Cradoc shrank from the anguish in Martin's face and voice as he gathered the harper into his arms. Cradoc picked up the book.

"It's safe," he said. "He brought it out."

He was not sure if Martin had heard him, but he saw his distress change to relief as he sought for and found Torquil's heartbeat.

"He went back in there to fetch it," Ferelith said. "And Cradoc. I should have helped, but I didn't dare."

Out of his newfound happiness, Cradoc grinned up at her.

"Just as well," he said. "It was quite nasty enough in there without having you to complicate it."

"Well—" Ferelith was beginning when a new voice dropped into the conversation.

"Good evening."

Cradoc sprang to his feet and spun around. Behind him was standing the dark man in the gray cloak.

"Good evening," he repeated. "I believe you've been looking for me."

Cradoc took a step back, clutching the book to him. "Oh, no, I haven't."

"Then you should have been, because I've been looking for you. Allow me to introduce myself; they call me the Mouse."

24

The next morning, in the Phoenix Inn, Cradoc and Ferelith had breakfast with the Mouse. Sunlight was pouring through the window. The danger of the night before seemed comfortably remote. In fact, apart from the vision of the Phoenix which Cradoc thought was etched on his mind forever, he found it difficult to remember what had happened.

Disconnected pictures were all that remained: Alys in the crowd around the fire, her terror giving way to joy when she learned that they and the book were safe; Martin's intent face as he examined Torquil's injuries; his own tunic sleeve slashed and soaked with blood where Rual's knife had found its mark; last of all, a cool, quiet room in the Phoenix where he could slide thankfully into sleep.

"But it can't be over," Cradoc objected. "Baric's men must still be looking for us."

The Mouse smiled thinly and shook his head.

"There's a rumor circulating that the book was burned last night in a fire from which the fugitives from Lindor barely escaped with their lives."

"Are you sure?" Ferelith asked.

"When I got home, my neighbor told me all about it. I saw no reason to contradict her."

He seemed quite certain and Cradoc had to accept what he said.

"What I don't understand," Cradoc went on, "is how you and Martin came to be at the fire."

"That's quite simple. Since I had word from Lord Herrian, I've been on the lookout for you. I saw you at the gate as I think you realized. But Baric's men were watching too, and I didn't dare speak to you. So I waited. Later I saw Torquil arrive with Martin. I know Martin—did he tell you?" His expression grew amused. "The wine trade from the Priory is very useful as wine casks can be used to bring in—or out—things other than wine."

"Books?"

The Mouse bowed his head.

"Exactly. So I followed Martin and your friend to the Phoenix. Then I went home. I expected Martin to send word to me. When I heard nothing, I came back here just in time to see you return. Shortly afterward I saw Martin leave. This time I managed to speak to him. He told me what had happened, and we went looking for Tybalt together. We didn't find him. We were still trying when we saw the fire. We didn't know it had anything to do with you. And in any case, we arrived too late to do anything. All the credit is yours."

He hesitated, sighed faintly, and went on, "Your task is over, but ours, perhaps, is only just beginning. Not everyone in the church will welcome your discovery. It will mean change and all of us are afraid of that."

Cradoc could understand. If someone had told him in that other life on Barren that he would come so far and do so much, fear itself might have prevented him.

"Meanwhile," the Mouse continued, "work has already started on the book. Only the outer edges were damaged. The text is still perfectly safe. You'll be able to take a consignment back with you to Barren before very long."

Cradoc smiled his gratitude.

"And in the meantime, if you want, you can stay with me. I'm always in need of another apprentice." He rose, draining his cup. "I must get back to work. Come and see me this afternoon. Martin will tell you where."

When he had gone, Cradoc and Ferelith finished their breakfast slowly. Cradoc had a strange, almost empty feeling. Their purpose had meant so much and now it was finished. He might almost have grieved if he had not realized that the end was a new beginning.

"I saw Alys this morning," Ferelith told him. "She'll stay here until I leave for Lindor. The innkeeper will make sure Tybalt can't get near her." She hesitated and then added, "I told her I was sorry—for not believing her. If she's going to serve my lady, we'll have to be friends."

"She might be a good friend."

Ferelith nodded, flushing a little and looking uncomfortable.

"I know. She did a good thing last night. So did Torquil. I shall have to tell him so, too." Briefly she looked close to laughter, or tears. "Cradoc, if you ever notice me getting too self-righteous again, just remind me about this, will you?"

Decisively she stood up.

"Let's go and find Torquil."

When Cradoc knocked at the door of the harper's room, it was Martin who answered. Torquil was in bed, propped up by pillows. He still looked frail and ill, but Cradoc thought he had never seen him so relaxed. Martin was sitting beside him, helping him with breakfast.

"Oh, Torquil, your hands!" Ferelith exclaimed.

Torquil glanced at his bandaged hands on the bedcover before him and gave a faint, contented smile.

"They'll heal," Martin said. "There'll be no lasting damage."

"I'm glad," Ferelith said and went on awkwardly. It was as if she were forcing herself to speak. "You were braver than me last night, Torquil. I didn't dare go back. I'm sorry I was unkind."

Torquil murmured something, looking embarrassed, and added, "I wasn't brave. I wasn't even thinking. Somehow I had to do it. And I never would have gotten out without Cradoc. Thank you for rescuing the harp."

Cradoc noticed the instrument for the first time sitting against the wall at the foot of the bed. And it also dawned on him that Torquil had put the book before the harp.

"I hardly knew I had rescued it," Cradoc admitted. "But I'm glad I did. After all, we brought the wretched thing, between us, all the way from Lindor. It would have been a pity to lose it before you even had the chance to play it."

"And when I've never even heard you," Martin added. He

looked around at all of them. "You've done very well, all three of you," he said. "The church and all the Six Worlds will be in your debt." Before they had time to feel embarrassed by his praise he went on briskly, "So what are you going to do now?"

"I'm going back to my lady," Ferelith replied promptly. "After all, that's why I came to Centre—not to go racketing around all over the planet with you, Cradoc Birdscarer."

Cradoc grinned at her affectionately.

"I'm going to work for the Mouse," he told Martin. "But when the first books are ready, I shall take some back to Barren. I want to study with Father Huon, to learn to read it for myself. And perhaps we'll build a church on Barren. And after that— well, perhaps that's enough to be going on with," he ended.

"And what about you, Torquil?" Ferelith asked.

Pure happiness flooded into Torquil's face.

"I'm going back to the Priory with Martin." The light died a little and he asked with something of his old shy hesitance, "If you're sure they'll want me?"

"They'll welcome you," Martin reassured him. "And with your music we'll give such praise to God as we've never known before."

"So we're to go our separate ways," Cradoc said. The empty feeling within him had intensified at the thought of losing friends he felt he had scarcely found.

"Everything comes to an end," Martin told him. "All the same," he added, "I find it hard to believe that the three of you won't see each other again. If I were a prophet, I would say that God still has tasks for you to do."

They were all silent for a moment, thinking about what that might mean. Martin began clearing away the remains of Torquil's breakfast. Suddenly the harper sat upright.

"Cradoc, your cross! You must take it back now."

Clumsily, with bandaged hands, he tried to take it off. Cradoc stopped him.

"No, keep it. I'd like you to. And Father Huon would like to think of it going to the Priory."

"Thank you." He hesitated and then went on. "Cradoc, we

did see Him, didn't we—the Lord Phoenix, in the fire?"

"Yes, we did." Sudden dismay seized him and he turned to Martin. "Martin, as soon as we got out, the roof fell in. The Phoenix was still there. Martin, He couldn't be destroyed like that, could He?"

Martin shook his head.

"Of course not. Our Lord chose that form to show Himself to you. But He isn't bound by it. Besides, have you forgotten everything that Father Huon told you? Come, I'll show you."

He led them down the stairs of the inn and out through the courtyard. Torquil came too, shaky but determined, leaning on Martin's arm. In daylight the way seemed shorter to the abandoned house which was now no more than a pile of blackened and smoking rubble. Martin picked his way across it carefully. Then he stopped, moving aside a charred piece of wood.

"Look."

Revealed in the ruins, pale in the midst of the blackness, were the shards of a great egg. Cradoc thought they still retained a faint translucence, as if reluctant to surrender the light they had imprisoned.

"He is risen," Martin said softly. "He is alive and free and with us in the world. Cradoc, nothing can destroy Him—nothing from now to the end of time."

Somewhere, just on the edge of sight, there was a flicker of golden wings.

Storm Wind

"I'm not going!"

The war had always been distant—nothing but newscast reports or stories from men home on leave. But now that the war is getting closer, Randal's mother is sending him to Altir—which is supposed to be safer—but he does not want to go. Determined that Altir will be boring and he'll detest his cousin, Randal quickly discovers that his expectations are anything but reality. He and his cousin Veryan soon find themselves far more involved in the fallout of the war than they ever dreamed they would be.

As the two journey through the city filled with destruction, Randal is faced with more decisions than he's faced in his life, one of which is the biggest decision he'll ever make—whether or not to take God seriously.

Visit a time when the Six Worlds were young, before their people lost contact with Earth, before the Black Years began, before it was dangerous to believe.

Cherith Baldry is involved with literature, especially children's books, in all aspects of her life. She is a teacher and school librarian and has two children of her own. She and her family live in England where she enjoys writing, reading, and gardening.

Chariot Books™
A Division of Cook Communications

Rite of Brotherhood

"You must do what you can to stop this war."

Aurion leaves his home on Two Islands as a hostage of the Tar-Askans, but he also goes to Tar-Askar as an ambassador.

The people of Tar-Askar have long-ago forsaken the ways of the peace-loving God of their ancestors, and now worship the god of power and war, Askar. Aurion is convinced that the way to prevent the war the Tar-Askans are preparing for is to turn them back to worshiping God. He plans to start with Arax, the king's son and his distant cousin. When he meets Arax, however, he wonders just how wise a choice he made.

The people of the Six Worlds long ago lost contact with Earth and the belief of its people. Journey through the Saga of the Six Worlds and discover, as they do, that what's gone may not always be for good.

Cherith Baldry is involved with literature, especially children's books, in all aspects of her life. She is a teacher and school librarian and has two children of her own. She and her family live in England where she enjoys writing, reading, and gardening.

Chariot Books™
A Division of Cook Communications

❖ PARENTS ❖